LOVE NOTES

Boys on the Brain
and Other Junior High Love Stories

♡ ♡ ♡

Karle Dickerson

Illustrated by Kurt Kress

Troll Associates

Table of Contents

Searching for Mr. Perfect

"I need a boyfriend," Lauren McKenna announced to the reflection in her bedroom mirror. The lanky girl in the mirror merely stared back, her thin, serious face framed by thick auburn hair.

"Not just any guy," Lauren went on. "Someone-to-die-for cute. Totally athletic. Nice. Interesting. Definitely romantic."

"Sounds perfect," Lauren's best friend, Janey Sorenson, said as she poked her head into Lauren's room. "When do I meet him?"

Lauren spun around. "Oh," she said, her hands flying up to her burning cheeks. "Janey! I thought you couldn't come over today. You said your mom and dad wanted you to rake leaves or something."

Janey plopped herself down in Lauren's gigantic beanbag chair. "I paid Curtis part of my allowance to play gardener for me. He's saving up to buy some toy called a Battle Toad. So who's this perfect guy?"

Lauren picked up her brush and ran it slowly through her hair. "I haven't met him yet," she said, frowning at her reflection and taking an angry swipe at her cowlick. "But I will."

Janey started to laugh. "At *our* school? I don't think so."

"Well, maybe not at school," Lauren said, giving up on her hair and applying some lip gloss. "But . . . somewhere."

Janey hoisted herself out of the chair. "It's the first day in weeks that it hasn't rained. Let's go play tennis or something!"

Lauren shook her head. "I'm not in the mood. I just kinda want to hang around here."

"Well, that's boring," Janey said, wrinkling her nose. "Just think about it—exercise equals a good body and a good mind, which all adds up to helping you attract Mr. Perfect."

"You go on," Lauren said. "I just feel like sitting around today."

Janey started toward the door. "Tell you what— you sit around dreaming about Mr. Perfect and I'm going to go play tennis. Who knows? Maybe I'll at least meet Mr. Okay out on the courts."

"You can have Mr. Okay," Lauren said. "I'm not settling for anything less than Mr. Perfect."

After Janey left, Lauren took over the beanbag chair, closed her eyes, and pictured her dream guy. He'd be tall, with muscled arms and strong legs— definitely someone who worked out. She wasn't sure whether he'd have straight black hair or dark brown curls, but she knew that his eyes would be blue and that he'd have a great smile. He wouldn't be into how he looked, but he'd dress well. And, of course, he'd be into sports—maybe basketball or baseball. Brains were important, too, so Lauren also pictured Mr. Perfect as a good student, someone who read a lot and wanted to talk about serious topics, like the environment and the homeless. His heart, Lauren thought, was probably most important. Yes, her Mr. Perfect would have a big heart with room for—

Suddenly, Lauren's own heart sank. "As if I'm ever going to meet anyone like that in real life," she mumbled to no one.

♡ ♡ ♡

The next morning as Lauren walked to school, she pretended that her fantasy guy was walking with her.

"That blue sweater really lights up your eyes," he'd say. Then he'd notice the new way she was wearing her hair. *"When your hair falls over your shoulders like that, you look even more beautiful."*

Lauren tilted her head back and gave her hair a slight shake, enjoying the feeling of it against her back.

"You got a bug in your hair or **something**," a deep voice said right behind her.

It was a real voice! Lauren quickly shook her head and a harmless ladybug flew out of her hair. Then she turned around to thank whoever had warned her. Great. It was Matt Stover, science nut. Since when did he start to walk this way to school?

7

Lauren took in his loose-fitting jeans and shapeless sweater and the long, casual way he walked. He was nothing like the guy of her dreams. She threw a quick "thanks" at him and continued walking.

Matt caught up with her. "You in a hurry?" he asked. He peered at his diving watch. "We've got 24 minutes and 34 seconds until school starts."

"I . . . I have to hit the library to finish a history paper," Lauren lied.

She sped up, and Matt dropped back. Lauren breathed a sigh of relief. She'd never meet the guy she really wanted if she spent her time talking idly with a bunch of Mr. Okays like Matt.

That afternoon in history, Lauren tuned out boring Mr. Trainor and his ridiculous imitation of Winston Churchill. Her mind started wandering, and soon her gaze turned to the guys around her. To her right sat total dweebazoid Steve Naylor. Then two rows up was superjock Richy Pressler. Half the girls in school were bonkers over him and didn't care if he was limited to monosyllabic sentences. Bob Vanderholt, sitting behind her, had some possibilities. If only she didn't have such vivid memories of his imitating train noises all the time in the fourth grade.

Lauren sighed and started sketching in her notebook. A handsome, rugged face took shape. She added a sweep of black hair and sat back to admire her creation. If only she could meet someone like that.

Then the bell rang. Lauren hastily closed the notebook and jammed it into her backpack.

"A bunch of us are heading to the mall after school today," called Lauren's friend Heather. "Wanna join us?"

Lauren shook her head. "Not today. But maybe next time."

"Come on," pleaded Janey, walking up to join Lauren. "It'll be fun."

"Thanks, but I just don't feel like it," Lauren said, wanting to say that malls were boring. They weren't swarming with Mr. Perfects, so why bother?

Janey put her hands on her hips. "You know, you've been totally draggy lately," she said. "What's going on?"

"Nothing," Lauren said.

She couldn't tell Janey she was hopelessly in love—hopelessly because the guy didn't even exist.

"It won't be any fun without you," Janey persisted. "Please come."

Lauren looked at the girls. They were a fun group. "Oh, all right," she said reluctantly. "But—"

"No buts about it," Janey said. Then suddenly she lowered her voice to whisper in Lauren's ear. "Some guys are going to meet us there."

Lauren rolled her eyes. What a waste! None of them would be half as cool as the guy in her drawing.

When they got to the mall, Lauren and her friends went over to the video arcade. Sure enough, there were about six or seven guys Lauren recognized from school, including Matt Stover. When he saw her, he handed the controls of the video game he was playing to another guy and came up to her.

"Uh, catch any bugs lately?" he asked shyly.

Lauren forced a smile. "No, I've switched from hair spray to bug spray."

Matt's face went blank.

"It's a joke," she said, noticing that he had a slight chip in one of his front teeth and that he needed a haircut. Matt relaxed and his smile was easy and friendly. In spite of herself, Lauren let her guard down and decided that it wouldn't be all that bad to talk with Matt . . . for a while, anyway.

As she and her friends started to walk around the mall, the guys in tow, Matt stayed stuck to Lauren's side like chewing gum.

At first they walked in silence. Finally, Lauren felt as though she just had to say something. "Malls are so boring," she managed.

Matt half nodded. "To some people," he said, nonchalantly. "But I'm never bored."

Lauren looked away. Trust Matt to be interested in what goes on in a mall. She suddenly wished she were anywhere else.

"Do you ever wonder who poses those mannequins?" Matt said, suddenly grabbing her sleeve and pointing at the display window at a jeans shop. "My arms would fall out of my sockets if they were bent like that poor guy's."

Lauren looked at the mannequin's impossible pose. Then she felt a smile creep across her face. "You're right," she said, starting to laugh. "He looks totally uncomfortable."

Matt nodded and imitated the mannequin.

They both cracked up.

Then Lauren pointed to a female mannequin and froze into the exact same stilted position. She could only hold it a moment before both she and Matt were doubled over, convulsing with laughter. They walked along behind the group, and every once in a while either she or Matt would strike a mannequin pose and laugh until the others thought they were definitely strange. But Lauren didn't care. Matt wasn't exactly Mr. Perfect, but he sure was Mr. Fun.

When the group finally wound up at the food court, Matt went off to buy a hot pretzel and said he'd bring Lauren one, too.

"I think he likes you," whispered Janey after he'd left.

Lauren watched Matt walk off with his easy gait. "Maybe," she said. "But he's not my type."

Janey looked at her friend and shook her head. "You know, I was watching him with you today. He used to be just Matt Stover, but he's changed. Maybe he filled out or something. Anyway, I heard he's a fantastic swimmer. What more do you want?"

Lauren shrugged. Janey would never understand. Her perfect guy wouldn't be buying her a pretzel at a shopping mall to show her how much he liked her. He'd take her window shopping so she could pick out something sophisticated. He'd be discussing movies, or books, or maybe even politics. He'd know some romantic spot away from screaming kids.

That evening when Lauren got home, she tore the picture of Mr. Perfect out of her notebook and tacked it on her bulletin board. "Where are you?" she asked the guy in the picture. "Will we ever meet?"

♡   ♡   ♡

The next day was Saturday. For some reason, Lauren had a feeling of expectation.

"Your eyes look all sparkly this morning," her mom said at the breakfast table.

"Is my little girl in love?" asked her dad.

"Dad!" Lauren exclaimed, rolling her eyes.

"You *are* in love, aren't you?" her younger sister, Cassie, teased.

"How about if everyone leaves Lauren alone?" her mother interrupted. She turned to Lauren. "So what are you going to do today, honey?" she said, trying not to sound as though she were prying, which Lauren knew she was.

Lauren chewed her waffle and closed her eyes. Mr. Perfect would pick her up, and they would head to the beach. Maybe they'd ride bikes on the boardwalk until dusk, then walk hand in hand along the pier. And then—

"Mom, look at her," Cassie said. "She looks like she does when she's watching some drippy romance movie for the zillionth time."

Lauren's eyes blazed. "I'm going to my room," she said, jumping up.

"No, you're not," her mother said firmly. "It's too nice outside to stay indoors. Call a friend and find something to do."

Lauren wanted to remind her mom that she was fourteen, not five, but something about the set of her mom's jaw made her think better of it.

Her first call went to Janey. "My brother's got a stupid baseball game," Janey had whined, "and I'm sentenced to the house to watch my baby sister."

Next she called Heather, then Monica, then Gail, but everyone seemed to have plans for the day. Dejected, Lauren hung up the phone. Now what? If she didn't think of something fast, her mom would try to talk her into taking Cassie somewhere. No way! She jumped up and headed for the garage to get her mountain bike.

A few minutes later she was flying along her street, the wind rushing through her hair and making her eyes water. And soon there he was—her gorgeous fantasy guy, cycling along right beside her. She lifted her chin and let her long hair ripple out behind her.

"Let's try a new bike trail today," he'd say. *"We'll stop at the base of Bishop's Peak and have a picnic, just the two of us, and—"*

"Slow down," called a voice behind her. It wasn't Mr. Perfect.

"Oh, no," Lauren muttered to herself, reluctantly braking. Matt Stover was pedaling toward her on a beat-up old bike. As he pulled up next to her she caught a whiff of chlorine.

"I was just riding home from swimming practice and I saw you," he said, still catching his breath. "What a coincidence."

Lauren smiled weakly. "Yeah, a coincidence," she said, thinking what an unlucky one it was. She eyed Matt's half-untucked shirt. Oh, well. No points for neatness.

"Where are you off to?" Matt asked, trying to sound casual.

Lauren shrugged. "Nowhere." She hoped she sounded boring enough that he'd just ride off. But no such luck.

"Mind if I ride with you?" he asked. "I can always use more of a workout."

"Sure," Lauren said, sighing inwardly. Mr. Perfect would have to wait until Mr. Science got lost.

"I know this totally cool bike path by the lake," Matt said eagerly. "It's not that crowded, so we can really fly."

"Great," said Lauren, trying to make the best of it. "Lead on."

Lauren found herself falling into a pedaling rhythm as she raced alongside Matt. He lifted his face and seemed to drink in the wind as he rode.

He always looks like he's having fun doing the simplest things, Lauren thought, forgetting about her Mr. Perfect for a while.

They stopped and bought some bottled water and snacks at a convenience store, then rode on. As they came up over the hill, Lauren caught a glimpse of the lake. The sunlight seemed to dance on the water.

"It's beautiful," she called to Matt as they turned their bikes onto the bike trail.

Matt nodded. "I like to come here to get away and think," he said. "It's kind of my secret."

All at once, Lauren felt shy. "Thanks for sharing it with me," she said, surprised by the tone in her voice. It sounded just a little too dreamy. She hoped Matt wouldn't get the wrong idea.

She fell back as Matt started pedaling and tried to daydream about Mr. Perfect, but the sun and the wind and the rhythm of their riding kept calling her back to reality. She watched Matt's broad, muscular back as he rode ahead of her. After a while, she noticed that he'd turned his head to the left and was looking intently at something. She let her gaze follow his, but she couldn't see anything. Suddenly, Matt stopped his bike so quickly that she almost crashed into him.

"Sorry," he said, pointing out toward the water. "Hey, do you see something out there?"

Lauren looked. "No," she said slowly. "What am I looking for?"

Matt squinted against the sun. "There *is* something out there!" he said, excitedly. Just then he jumped off his bike and ran toward the beach. Kicking off his shoes, he plunged into the water.

Lauren watched, perplexed, as he started swimming in strong, steady strokes. *Weird,* she thought. Well, Janey was right about one thing: He definitely was a good swimmer. *But what was he doing?*

Suddenly, she saw a dog's head bobbing in the water. Matt was swimming as fast as he could, right for it. But couldn't dogs swim? Still, this one did seem to be having trouble. It disappeared, then reappeared. Lauren felt her breath catch. The poor dog was awfully far out there.

Lauren pulled the two bikes off the trail and ran out onto the beach. As she watched Matt swim closer and closer to the dog, she heard squeaking noises in the bushes next to her. Lauren felt the hair rise on the back of her neck. Gingerly, she kneeled down and pulled back the bushes. There, nestled in a corner, were three wriggling black shapes. "Puppies!" she cried. "That must be your mother out there."

She stood up and turned back to the lake. "Come on, Matt!" she cried. "You can do it!"

In a moment, Matt had reached the dog and was heading toward shore, pushing the dog along in front of him. He was also holding something above the water. Lauren shielded her eyes from the sun. What was he carrying? As he got closer, she saw

17

that it was another puppy! The mother dog was soon safely on the beach. She panted heavily, her dark eyes turning anxiously toward the puppy Matt was gently setting on the sand beside her.

"Matt, are you okay?" Lauren called, anxiously running over to him.

Matt sat down heavily on the sand, his hair falling forward and dripping in seaweedlike tendrils over his forehead.

"Yeah," he said breathlessly.

Lauren suddenly felt an urge to cry. Together they watched the dog as she licked her exhausted puppy.

"How do you suppose it happened?" Lauren asked, sinking down in the sand beside Matt.

"I have no idea," he said. "But at least there was a happy reunion."

"Thanks to you," Lauren said, noticing that his eyes were deep blue, almost the color of the lake in front of them. Then she heard the squeaking noises. How could she have forgotten the family in the bushes? "Take a look over there," Lauren said, pointing to where the puppies were.

As if on cue, the dog picked up the puppy in her mouth and made her way over to the bushes. Matt got up and took a peek at the happy brood.

"Those pups look like they're just a couple of weeks old," he said. "The mother has a collar but the tags are gone. Someone must be missing this little family. We ought to see if we can find the owner."

They spent a couple of hours knocking on the doors of homes around the lake. Finally, they located the owner of the dog family. He was a grumpy old man whose face lit up like a Christmas tree when Matt and Lauren explained why they were there.

Lauren rode quietly alongside Matt on their way home that afternoon. She thought about the day. It hadn't been boring at all—not for a minute. In fact, it had been perfect.

"You know, you're a pretty nice person," she said impulsively as they neared her house.

Matt slowed and turned to look at her. "So are you," he said softly. "I've thought so for a long time. You've always seemed like . . . like this perfect girl to me."

Lauren felt little fireflies of electricity sparking through her whole body. Then Matt smiled that special smile of his, the one that showed his slightly chipped, slightly imperfect tooth. Lauren answered with a smile of her own.

Suddenly, she knew that her search for Mr. Perfect was over.

The Summer School Blues

"I'll die this summer without you guys," Diane said sadly.

It was late afternoon, and Diane had spent the first day of her summer vacation becoming totally depressed, watching her best friends, Molly and Lisa, finish packing for camp. They were going on and on about all the fun they were going to have. Diane was going to be stuck here in boring old Montrose.

"We'll miss you, too," Lisa said as she struggled to zip her duffel bag. "But we'll only be gone for eight weeks."

"Eight weeks!" Diane wailed.

"We'll write all the time," Molly said, "and I promise that we'll talk about you so much to the guys at camp that they'll be dying to meet you next summer."

Next summer, thought Diane. That might as well be forever! This summer was now, and it was going to be terminally dull. But she didn't want to make her friends feel bad. After all, it wasn't their fault she was in this mess. She helped her friends lug their heavy duffel bags out to the car.

As she watched them leave, Diane waved and tried to smile, but she had a hard time holding back the tears. If only she had kept up her grades in English! If only she hadn't gotten so caught up in rehearsing for the leading role in the spring play! Then she wouldn't be stuck going to summer school to bring up her grade. Instead, she'd be on her way to Camp Washoe with her friends, where they'd all be counselors-in-training. When she got home, her orange marmalade cat, Fat Max, jumped on her lap. Diane hugged Max and cried and cried.

♡ ♡ ♡

A week later Diane was getting ready for the first day of summer school. She considered trying to wrangle her explosion of hair into a braid, but decided to forget it. What was the point in looking good? No one she knew was going to summer school. She slipped down to the kitchen and grabbed an apple for breakfast. Her mom walked in, her briefcase under her arm.

"Good morning, punkin," she said.

Diane scowled at her mother's warm smile.

"Don't be so glum," her mother said. "You may surprise yourself and like summer school. In any case, you need to make up that grade."

Diane knew her mother was right, but as she set off for school, she couldn't help thinking about the fun her friends were probably already having at camp. Molly was so cute and bubbly that she probably had six boyfriends by now. And Lisa was probably flirting like mad. Diane felt she would be lucky to find a single guy worth flirting with all summer.

She was feeling sorry for herself and walking with her head down when suddenly she bumped full on into someone. Her head snapped up as that someone grabbed her by the shoulders and said, "Whoa. Easy there."

Startled, she looked into a pair of brown eyes— the boring brown eyes of Bruce Hollinger. She'd seen him around school, but she'd never really talked to him before. Everyone said he always had his nose in a history book.

"Uh, sorry," she muttered, then pulled away.

"No problem," he said with an easy tone. "I should have been looking where I was going." He shrugged and bent down to pick up the book he'd dropped when they collided.

Diane glanced at the title: *Montrose—A Town Undiscovered.* "What a boring title," she said, thinking *"undiscovered" is right, because there's nothing here to discover.*

"Listen, I'm late for class," she said, running off.

When she got to Ms. Hutchins's classroom, Diane looked around to see whether she could spot someone she knew. But no such luck. None of the people she knew were the type that hang around town and go to summer school. Ugh . . . it was going to be a long summer.

As the bell rang, Diane saw Bruce slip into class. He walked over and sat down next to her.

"Hi," he said, plunking his backpack onto his desk. "So you're sentenced to a summer in Ms. Hutchins's English class, too, huh?"

"Yeah," Diane said flatly, then turned to look out the window. The last thing she wanted to do was make conversation with a history buff. If only someone new, someone with personality, would sit next to her!

"Let's begin, class," said Ms. Hutchins. "We have a full summer ahead of us. "I've prepared these book lists and essay assignments to help you challenge yourselves. You can all benefit from spending more time reading and writing and less time watching television."

"Buried alive by books," Diane grumbled aloud.

Bruce grabbed his throat and pretended to choke. "Help me! Help! Attack of the killer books!"

Diane shot him a warning look as Ms. Hutchins narrowed her eyes.

"See me after class, Mr. Hollinger," the teacher said sternly.

Diane actually found herself feeling sorry for Bruce. After all, he was only trying to have some fun. She hoped Ms. Hutchins wouldn't be too hard on him.

When she got home, Diane headed to the refrigerator for a snack before tackling her homework. She was supposed to write a descriptive essay, but how could she be descriptive when she was totally depressed? She saw that the mail was on the kitchen table, with two postcards from Camp Washoe right on top. "Great," she mumbled, wolfing down a cookie and picking up the first card. "Now I can read about the wonderful time I'm not having."

The card from Lisa showed the woodsy surroundings of the camp mess hall. Diane felt a lump in her throat. It looked so familiar, and it brought back so many memories of other summers.

"Dear D," Diane read. *"I can't stand it. We're having too much fun! We've been swimming every day. Molly's already in love. Everyone's asking where you are. Write. Love, Lisa"*

Diane made a face, then picked up the next postcard. This one showed Lake Washoe at dawn.

"Diane!" it said. *"Don't believe Lisa for a minute. It's been raining since we got here. It's the worst. The lake will probably flood our cabins by tomorrow. I almost wish I were home in Montrose. At least the food would be better. Wish you were here to make us laugh. XOXOXO, Molly"*

Diane couldn't help smiling. Good old Molly— she always tried to make her feel better. But today it just wasn't enough. Really depressed now, Diane went slowly up the stairs to her room.

Sitting at her desk and staring out the window, Diane tried to think of what to write about, but nothing was coming to her. Finally, she wrote about how hard it is to write an essay when you're thinking about roasting marshmallows around a campfire.

The next day, Diane turned in her essay, then leaned her head tiredly on her books. She watched disinterestedly as Bruce entered the classroom.

"Hey," he said casually. "What's the matter? You look fried."

Diane sat up and rubbed her eyes. "Oh," she said with a shrug. "I stayed up kind of late working on my essay."

"Trying to earn brownie points?" he asked, his eyes twinkling.

"I wish! I'll be lucky if she can even read my handwriting."

Bruce laughed. "Oh, I'm sure she'll manage," he said.

Diane found herself looking Bruce over. Okay, so maybe he didn't knock a girl's socks off in the looks department, but if she had to pass the time talking with someone, it might as well be him.

"By the way, did you get into trouble yesterday?" she asked.

Bruce grinned and shook his head. "No," he said in a low voice. "She just lectured me about taking this class seriously."

When the bell rang, Ms. Hutchins assigned the class *another* essay, due at the end of the week.

"Doesn't she think we have anything to do this summer?" Bruce grumbled under his breath as they left class.

"Well, she's got me figured out, anyway," Diane said. "I *don't* have anything better to do."

26

Bruce paused and cocked his head as he looked at her. "A great-looking girl like you doesn't have anything to do this summer?" he asked.

Diane stared straight ahead, taking in his compliment. Funny, it didn't sound like it was Bruce talking. She shielded her eyes from the strong sunlight as they stepped out onto the school's front steps.

"Well," she said slowly, "I would have had something better to do, but I let my English grade slip this year, so I'm stuck here. I could have been with my friends at camp. And we'd be water-skiing, and riding horses and playing tennis and hanging out by the lake, and—"

She stopped. He probably couldn't care less, anyway.

Bruce shifted his backpack. "You mean you'd rather be having fun with your friends than writing essays for Ms. Hutchins?"

Diane stared at Bruce for a second, then she realized he was joking. She smiled. "I know—it's hard to believe, isn't it?"

"There's nothing I'd rather be doing," Bruce said, trying not to smile.

Diane stopped and looked at Bruce—really looked at him. "What *would* you really rather be doing?" she asked, actually interested.

Bruce shrugged and continued walking with his long, easy stride. "Actually, I don't mind hanging around here," he said. "Before we moved to Montrose, we used to move around a lot because of

27

my father's job. I never lived in the same home for more than a few months or stayed very long at the same school. We've been here almost two years now. It feels like home, and I'm kind of glad to just sort of stick around."

Diane wondered if Bruce were joking. But he wasn't. *Weird,* she thought. *Someone who actually prefers to be in Montrose.*

"Well, there's no history here," she said. "It's just a small town with a couple of mini-malls and pizza places and not much else. It has to be the most boring place on earth."

Bruce shook his head. "Not to me, it isn't. I was actually reading about the history of Montrose until this gigantic reading list landed in my lap."

"Yeah, it was pretty heavy, wasn't it?" Diane said, feeling so much at ease with Bruce she couldn't believe she was actually interested in what she asked him next. "So, Mr. Montrose History Buff—what's new to do around this old town?"

"Lots of things," Bruce said.

"Name one!" Diane challenged him.

"Have you ever gone rollerblading around the park at sunset?" he asked, his eyes locking with hers.

Diane looked away, suddenly feeling uncomfortable at Bruce's intensity. She shook her head.

"Come with me after dinner," he said. "I'll meet you at seven."

He walked away, not giving Diane a chance to say no.

Diane turned and headed for home. She had a funny feeling that even if he had given her a chance to think it over, she would have said yes, anyway.

♡ ♡ ♡

After dinner, Diane grabbed her rollerblades and skated to the park. As Bruce skated up to meet her he called, "Come on! You should see this boring old town from the top of this hill. You can see all the way to the ocean."

They skated to the top of the hill and looked down on the panorama below. Diane had to admit she'd never thought about how different Montrose might look from so high. "Thanks for showing me this," she said to Bruce, looking into his chocolate-brown eyes.

Bruce cuffed her playfully, then took off on his skates. "Race you back down," he said. "Last one to the statue has to write an essay!"

Diane laughed and quickly took off after him.

♡ ♡ ♡

That night, Diane's mom handed her two more postcards from Camp Washoe. The first one she read was from Lisa.

"*Dear Summer School Scholar,*" Lisa wrote. "*I am having the worst time trying to decide between Michael and David. In between, I am water-skiing and leading the camp sing-along. It's stopped raining. Oh, I wish you were here. Love, Lisa"*

Molly's note was a little longer. She described the training the would-be counselors were getting, then she dashed off a line or two about the sunset over the lake. Diane thought about what Ms. Hutchins always said: Memorize a scene with all five senses. It seemed to her that Molly could have used more descriptive imagery. Inspired to follow Ms. Hutchins's advice in her own writing, Diane went to work on her essay. She closed her eyes and recalled the sights, sounds, and smells of standing next to Bruce on the hill in the park.

At the end of the week, Ms. Hutchins asked for the essays.

"What was yours about?" Bruce whispered to Diane.

"A sunset," Diane said.

"Mine, too," replied Bruce.

When Ms. Hutchins returned the essays the next week, Diane had gotten an A. She leaned over to Bruce and asked him what he had gotten.

Grinning from ear to ear, he held up his paper to show her he'd gotten the same grade. "Celebration time?" he asked, and seeing Diane's enthusiastic nod he added, "Then ice cream sundaes at Delaney's it is. Okay with you?"

"Sure," Diane said. Then, suddenly, she felt let down. After all, what was she getting all excited about? She'd been to Delaney's a hundred zillion times before. Okay, Bruce seemed nice enough, and they did have a lot of fun rollerblading, but basically he was just another guy from her hometown. Hardly anything like the cute, interesting guys she'd be meeting if she were at camp. How could she have allowed herself to end up in Montrose in July? Dee-pressing!

Still, when they were walking to Delaney's later, Diane found that she didn't feel all that upset anymore. In fact, she was starting to feel, well, okay. Montrose in July wasn't all that bad, she thought.

"Hey!" Bruce exclaimed, stopping in front of an old brick building with two white pillars at the entrance. "This is the Montrose Historical Society. Do you mind if we go in? I've always wanted to check this place out."

Diane shrugged. "Why not?"

They walked inside the musty old building and made their way over to a glass case filled with musty old trophies.

"It's too quiet in here," Diane whispered. "It gives me the creeps."

"That's because there are the ghosts of a thousand souls in here," Bruce answered in a theatrical whisper. He ran his fingers up her spine to give her the chills.

Diane shivered—was it because of what Bruce just did, or because he'd suddenly taken her hand to pull her over to a wall covered with old, sepia-toned

photographs? He read the photo display title out loud: "The pioneers come to Montrose."

The photos showed solemn men, women, and children next to their wagons. Their eyes pulled Diane into the picture. "These people look so full of hope," she whispered to Bruce.

Bruce whispered back, "Yeah, and they were coming to Montrose. Maybe they knew there was something going on here!"

They walked around the museum, looking at photographs that depicted the harsh winters and droughts of past years.

"Times sure were tough here," Diane noted.

Bruce nodded. "Things are so much easier now." He paused and looked at her. "Do you like looking at historical stuff like this?" he asked.

Diane thought about that for a second. "I didn't think so, but it's kind of neat. It's strange to think that Montrose has been around for so long."

"Yeah," said Bruce. "And it wasn't always known as Montrose, either. It used to be called 'Valley of the Bears.'"

"Wow," Diane said, amazed. "I didn't know that."

They made their way to the front desk and signed the guest book. As they began to leave, Diane noticed a rack of historical postcards. She picked out two, one for Molly and one for Lisa. Then she and Bruce stepped out onto the sidewalks of modern Montrose once again.

"Tell you what," Bruce said as they approached Delaney's. "Let's get cones to go. I feel like walking."

Diane nodded her agreement, and soon they were happily walking and talking and looking in all the windows along the main street.

"This ice cream is delicious!" Diane exclaimed. She felt a little silly as soon as she'd said it—it was ordinary ice cream, after all, and she *had* been to Delaney's a hundred zillion times. Suddenly, she stopped and looked at Bruce. "Do you know what? I think Delaney's is standing right on the spot where the general store used to be in old Montrose. I saw it in one of the photographs."

"And there's where the livery stable used to be," Bruce said, pointing to an Italian restaurant as they passed by.

"The blacksmith's shop was right where the video store is now," Diane said. Then she took Bruce's hand. "You know," she confessed, "I was sure that this summer was going to be the worst ever. Here I was, stuck in boring old Montrose. But somehow, it's all changed. When you really get to know it, Montrose is anything but boring."

Bruce smiled. "I can't imagine that anyplace would be boring with you in it," he said gently. "You've made being stuck in summer school not such a bad thing."

Diane let the good feeling wash over her. It was warmer than any feeling she'd be getting by playing in the sun at Camp Washoe. It was warmer than any other guy could be making her feel in any camp or any town anywhere on earth. Lisa and Molly couldn't possibly be having this much fun, Diane thought. And somehow, the long weeks of summer stretching out ahead didn't seem too long anymore. Now they seemed too short. After all, Diane had all of Montrose to explore . . . and best of all, she'd be exploring it with Bruce Hollinger!

Boys on the Brain

"So what am I supposed to do about David?"
Trisha Marcus asked, studying her profile in the restroom mirror. "I mean, what did I ever do to make a guy like *him* like me?"

Mary Gonzales watched her new friend fussing with her makeup. Why did Trisha and half the girls at school worry so much about what they looked like? But Mary already knew the answer: boys.

"Why are you asking me stuff about boys?" Mary answered her friend with what she felt was the most logical response. She couldn't help but sound a little annoyed. Her brain was occupied with other things. She didn't have boys on the brain like every other girl in her school. "I don't understand anything about people liking each other anyway, so why ask me?"

Trisha frowned. "I'm asking you because your mom writes about love and stuff," she said. "Excuse me, but I figured you might know."

Mary wished that her mom did *anything* but write romance novels for a living. "Look, I don't know where my mom gets all her answers," she said matter-of-factly. "I just know *I* don't have any."

Love—it was spreading all over school like a sickness. First Mary's former best friend, Kristi, got hit by it. Ever since she'd gotten a boyfriend she'd barely talked to Mary. Then it hit Lisa. Once she'd started liking Carl Fredericks, all she talked about was what she should wear to impress him. Now it was Trisha who was going all boy crazy. Mary could hardly stand it.

"It's not that there's anything wrong with David," Trisha stated as they walked down the hall on their way to class. "I just like Bobby Porter more. And now the Valentine's Day dance is coming up. What if David asks me before Bobby?"

Mary ignored Trisha's question. "That's another thing I don't understand—Valentine's Day. A whole day devoted just to love? Yuck!"

They walked into computer class and sat down at their terminals.

Mary saw David lurking near Trisha like a shark. As her friend helplessly endured David's puppy-dog gaze, Mary felt sorry for both of them. Love was just annoying.

When the bell rang, Mr. Korns called the class to order. He gave them data to input as a warm-up exercise and then passed out a speed-inputting contest. Mary just loved contests like that. In fact, she loved anything that had to do with computers.

One by one, other students were eliminated. Mary pressed on, and soon realized that she and David were the only two left in the running. The game went on for another fifteen minutes with neither one missing a keystroke. Finally, Mr. Korns pronounced them co-winners, presenting them each with a certificate for a free slice of pizza and a soda at Planet Pizza.

"Congrats," David said loping along after Mary and Trisha as they left class. "You were great, Mary. How'd you get so good on the computer?"

"I've had lots of practice," Mary said curtly. She didn't want to be rude, but she did hope David would stop trying to flirt with Trisha through her. Couldn't he see that Trisha wasn't paying any attention to him?

"What kind of practice?" David persisted, his eyes locking onto Mary's as though he were seeing her for the first time.

Mary shrugged. She looked away so she wouldn't have to look into his intense dark eyes. "I use my dad's laptop most of the time," she said. "It's pretty fast. My mom's got this big, clunky older model. She talks about getting rid of it, but she never does."

Trisha suddenly poked her in the side and whispered, "What are you talking to him for? He'll never go away."

Mary glared at her friend. How could she be so insensitive? She felt sorry for David, who was suddenly looking very uncomfortable. Then he mumbled something about having to be somewhere and walked away.

"Isn't Bobby Porter cute?" Trisha said breathlessly, as though nothing had happened. She tugged

39

Mary's sleeve and pointed to the lanky dark-haired boy rounding the corner. "Now how can I get him to ask me to the dance?"

"Is that all you think about?" Mary snapped at her friend. "Guys, Valentine's Day, and love? I'm sick of all of it." She walked off, feeling kind of silly for having gotten so excited about the whole thing. She felt even sillier when she found herself thinking about David and Trisha all afternoon. It just didn't make sense. David was too logical for this. Why couldn't he see that he was totally wasting his time with a girl like Trisha? He was levelheaded and quiet. Trisha was loud and flighty. They were a total mismatch.

Mary thought about David and Trisha the rest of the afternoon, all through dinner, and into the evening. She didn't know why it bothered her so much, and she decided to consult the love expert—her mom.

She walked into her mother's study and plopped down on the overstuffed couch, rolling her eyes at the posters of her mom's book covers mounted all over the walls. The study was like a shrine to romance—definitely not a subject Mary would be interested in surrounding herself with. She watched her mom at the computer monitor. She was muttering "deep, smoldering eyes" over and over. Finally, Mary couldn't stand it and interrupted her.

"Mom," she blurted out, "why do guys like girls who would never in a jillion years like them back?"

Her mom stopped muttering and looked up from her keyboard to stare dreamily at the poster of her first book cover hanging on the wall directly in front of her computer. It was a watercolor of a southern belle hugging a handsome hero in a uniform. The cover always made Mary sick to her stomach. Talk about mush!

"Love doesn't make sense," her mom said slowly, her eyes misting over. "I think it was a writer named Pascal who said, 'The heart has its reasons which reason knows nothing of.'"

Now Mary was sure she was going to be sick. "What's that supposed to mean?" she asked, not sure she really wanted to know.

Her mom smiled mysteriously. "Simply that feelings like love aren't easy to understand. They don't follow any logic, any pattern of reason, and—wait just a minute!" she said, her face lighting up. "You've given me an idea." She leaned over, kissed the top of Mary's head, and started typing rapidly. "I'm sorry, honey. Just let me get this down, and then we'll really talk."

Mary knew that when her mom was on a creative roll, nothing short of a fire in the house would get her to stop. Sighing, she got up and wandered out to the office her dad had set up for himself in the garage. This was definitely more her style. It was high-tech, streamlined, and efficient—not all messy and full of sappy love posters.

Her dad was calculating something on his computer and humming. "What's up, sweetie?" he asked, not pausing as he keyed in figures.

Mary watched the screen for a few seconds, trying to see whether she could beat the computer at the calculations. Normally, mental exercises like these were engrossing to her, but tonight thoughts of David kept crowding in and disturbing her concentration.

"Oh, nothing," she said, wandering off to do her homework.

But that night she dreamed something odd. She was dancing at the Valentine's Day dance with—of all people!—David Adler.

"Dumb," she said to herself as she brushed her teeth the next morning. There was no way she was going to start liking David. It was totally illogical to like someone if he liked someone else. As she got dressed and found herself *still* thinking about him, she resolved to be cool and logical the whole day, making sure to keep all thoughts of the Valentine's Day dance—and especially of David—banished from her mind.

♡ ♡ ♡

Mary and Trisha got to computer class early that morning. "You're in luck," Mary whispered. "Lover boy has yet to arrive."

But then, as if on cue, in walked David.

Unable to help herself, Mary's eyes went right

to him, and she quickly noticed that his eyes were moving right to Trisha. Without hesitating, David walked over to her desk and put a badly wrapped box next to her computer.

"I brought you a present," he said to Trisha, sliding the box closer. "It's for your computer."

Trisha tore off the paper and pulled a fuzzy mouse-shaped thing out of the box. She looked at it, then at David. "Thanks," she said, looking puzzled.

It was obvious that Trisha didn't care for David or his present. She probably didn't even know what David had given her. Mary couldn't help feeling sorry for him. "Great mouse cover," she said, trying to help the poor guy out. "That's so clever. A mouse for a computer mouse."

David shot her a look of gratitude.

"Oh, I get it," Trisha said, without enthusiasm. "You put this fuzzy thing on top of your computer mouse."

"Affirmative," David said, beaming, then suddenly he looked embarrassed when he saw Trisha's boy-are-you-a-nerd expression. "I . . . I mean, right, it's for your computer mouse."

Mary watched him slouch into his seat, then she turned to Trisha. "You could have been nicer," she whispered.

"But I don't even have a computer at home," Trisha replied. "And anyway, I sure don't want to give him any wrong ideas."

"You really should just tell David you're not

interested in him," Mary said. "It's all perfectly logical. Just put the guy out of his misery."

Trisha looked at Mary. "I can't," she said, gloomily. Then her face brightened. "But if it's all so logical to you, why don't you tell him for me?" She dangled David's present in front of Mary's nose. "If you do, I'll give you my fuzzy little mouse cover," she added cajolingly.

Mary took the mouse and turned it over and over in her hand. She really thought it was a nice gift: Perfect for . . . well, her.

"Oh, keep it anyway," Trisha said. "I sure don't have any use for it."

Mary held it up to her cheek and felt the softness against her skin. It would be kind of cute sitting on a mouse at home. "Thanks," she said. "I'll see what I can—"

But Trisha didn't hear her. She was too busy drooling over Bobby Porter, who'd just come into class.

♡ ♡ ♡

That evening, Mary sat at her dad's computer and put the mouse cover on his mouse. When he came into the office, he noticed it right away

"What's this rodent doing on my equipment?" he asked, raising an eyebrow.

"It doesn't really serve any purpose," Mary said, almost embarrassed. "But it's cute, isn't it?"

"Cute?" her dad asked. "I've never known you to waste any time on cute."

"Dad," she said, swiveling around in his chair. "Did you ever have to tell someone that someone he was interested in didn't like him?"

Her dad scratched his head. "No," he admitted. Then he cleared his throat nervously. "You have boy problems, don't you?"

"*I* don't have boy problems," Mary said quickly. "But Trisha sure does."

Her dad looked uneasy. "Then let her solve them." He thought for a moment. "Or better yet, talk with your mom and see what she says. She's the expert around here on matters of the heart."

"Well, I would," Mary said slowly. "But your answers about things are usually more logical. I'm like you, Dad. I'd rather not get all mushy about this love business."

Her dad grinned. "Logic and love don't always mix," he said, "and sometimes it doesn't hurt to get all mushy about this love stuff."

"That's what Mom always says," Mary said, wondering why her dad had such a silly look on his face.

"Well, if you ask me," said her dad, "your mom is pretty logical when it comes to matters of love." He paused for just a moment. "Now scoot. It's late, and you've got school tomorrow."

When Mary walked into computer class the following day, she noticed that David was already there. He looked up at her and smiled warmly.

"Trisha's got a dentist appointment," Mary said quickly.

"I know. She told me yesterday that she was going to miss class," David said. "She also told me that she gave you the mouse cover."

Mary looked down at her sneakers. "I—uh—hope you don't mind."

"It's got a good home," he said, shrugging his shoulders carelessly.

"Yeah," Mary said. "I'll make sure to keep it warm and fed."

David laughed. "Thanks," he said. "Tuck it in bed at night, too. Okay?"

For a moment, there was an awkward silence between them. "Hey, did I tell you my dad's computer has this new turbo feature?" Mary asked.

David's face lit up. And before Mary knew it, they were talking nonstop until class began.

At lunch, Mary was going to tell Trisha what a nice guy David was and that maybe she should give him a chance. But Trisha had big news.

"Guess what?" Trisha gushed. "Bobby Porter asked me to the Valentine's Day dance!"

Mary absorbed the information for a minute. "That's great," she said slowly. "But what about David? He's going to get hurt."

Trisha shrugged. "Well, at least he'll get the message when he sees me with Bobby, right? Now neither of us has to tell him."

Mary suddenly felt like telling her friend off.

Why couldn't she just be honest with the guy? She started to say something, but Bobby was walking toward them, and she knew Trisha would be a lost cause.

♡ ♡ ♡

That night, Mary helped her dad prepare dinner.

"Your mom's having a tough time coming up with an ending for her novel," her dad said. "She asked me to help, but it really has me stumped. Seems there's this woman named Talia who doesn't have a clue that this guy named Carl is in love with her. But the real problem is that Talia is nuts for Carl, too, but she doesn't even know it!"

Mary stirred some noodles on the stove. "Talia sounds totally dumb to me," she said. She didn't want to be talking about someone else's romance problems—especially if they weren't real. "Did I tell you that Trisha's going to the Valentine's Day dance with Bobby Porter?"

Her dad looked up from the meatballs he was making. "So why do you look so sad?"

Mary searched for an answer, but her feelings were all tangled. "There aren't any storybook endings in real life, are there, Dad?" she asked suddenly.

Her dad smiled. "Sometimes there are," he said. "You'll see."

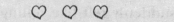

The next day, Trisha blabbed all the way to school about what she would wear to the dance. Mary thought she might actually scream and was glad when they walked into computer class. But as she sat staring at her screen, she realized she felt upset, though for the life of her she couldn't figure out why. Suddenly, she looked up to see David looking at her.

"Well?" he asked.

"Well what?" she asked him back.

"Did the mouse sleep well?"

Mary laughed. "He had kind of a restless night," she said. David was pretty cute. She hated to see him hurt. She just had to tell him right now—it wasn't right for him to go on loving somebody who was in love with someone else.

"David, Trisha's going with Bobby Porter to the Valentine's Day dance." The words tumbled out of her mouth.

She waited to see a pained look appear on David's face. He smiled instead. "I know," he said, glancing over at Trisha. "She told me."

"Are you okay?" Mary asked, surprised Trisha had gotten up the guts.

David shrugged. "At first I wasn't." He paused and looked at the floor, then back at Mary. "But then I realized that I wanted to ask someone else to the dance anyway."

"Who?" Mary heard the word escape from her mouth before she could stop it. It was none of her business who he wanted to ask out.

"I'm not telling yet," David said, grinning as he walked away.

Mary felt her cheeks flame. Her brain scrambled for a logical reason why she had asked him that in the first place. She quickly turned on her computer and logged in.

As the screen lit up, Mary saw some words flash before her.

MESSAGE UNREAD: ONE

Mary hit the enter key, and to her amazement, the following words appeared, together with a big heart.

TO MARY GONZALES, FROM DAVID ADLER

Below, a question popped up:

WILL YOU COME WITH ME
TO THE VALENTINE'S DAY DANCE?

Mary felt a warm glow radiate through her. All at once the confusion she'd been feeling lately disappeared. But when had David started liking *her*? And when exactly had she started to like him so much that her heart was beating as fast as it was? She laughed to herself. So what if there weren't logical answers to all questions!

She looked up from her screen to see David staring at her. "Look at your screen," she said, as she typed in her answer:

AFFIRMATIVE

At least this time, she thought, love and logic were mixing together very well.

Flirt City

"I can't stand it," Katie Paulsen said to her best friend, Hilary, before school Monday morning. She shook her head dramatically, and her curly, red hair bounced. "It's the worst thing that's ever happened to me. My little brother won the championship on the 'The Glop Show.'"

"Wow! What did he win?" asked Hilary.

"A computer," Katie said. Just then the bell rang, and they headed for their lockers. "He also won a college scholarship."

Hilary stopped dead in her tracks. "Glop, glop, glop," she said, chanting the show's impossibly stupid opening line. "I suppose Kevin's totally impossible to live with now."

Katie nodded bleakly. "Worse than ever. "Do you know what he said to me? He said, 'And you always thought *you* were going to be the TV star in the family. Well, *I* beat you to it.' And my parents said he could have this huge party next week when the show airs. Can you believe it? All his twerpy little friends will be there. I don't think I'll be able to stand it."

She threw open her locker. Just before the flying door banged against the other lockers, Mr. Finnerty, the drama teacher, caught it.

"Save that energy for tryouts for the spring play!" he said, smiling.

"I will, Mr. Finnerty," Katie said. But when he was gone she turned to Hilary. "Like I feel like trying out for anything anymore, now that my brother's the star." She fought back tears. "I never get any good parts, anyway."

Hilary gave Katie a look of support and patted her shoulder. "Well, *I* think you're star material. Just go for it."

Katie smiled in spite of herself. "Thanks, Hilary," she said.

"Don't look now, but here comes Hunt Morrison," Hilary said, leaning closer to Katie.

Katie thought Hunt was the cutest guy in school. He sat in front of her in Spanish class, but she'd never had the nerve to talk to him.

"Hey, Hil, Katie," Hunt said. He stopped and adjusted his backpack a few feet away from them.

"Hi, Hunt," Hilary said. "*Say hi!*" she whispered out of the corner of her mouth to Katie.

Katie gave Hilary a strangled look, then waited until she thought Hunt had walked on. "Is he gone?" she whispered frantically.

"Yes," Hilary said, shaking her head in exasperation. "I've said it before, and I'll say it again. You need to get over your terminal shyness."

"I know, I know," Katie said as she shut her locker. "It's just that he's so cool, I feel like an idiot around him."

"I think he seems interested in you," Hilary said. "All you need to do is flirt a little with him."

Just *thinking* about Hunt made Katie's heart do jumping jacks. Flirting was totally out of the question!

In any case, Katie was too busy obsessing over her little brother's stardom to think about flirting. "It isn't fair," she mumbled to herself as she walked to Spanish class just before lunch. *She* was supposed to be the star. She'd worked so hard on her drama lessons. All her dweeby little brother had done was send a card with his name on it to a game show, and poof! You'd think he'd just won an Oscar.

But once she was sitting in Spanish class, Katie started thinking about Hunt again. Julie Taylor was leaning over from the next seat and talking to him. Katie looked away and tapped her pencil on her desk. If only she could get up the nerve to talk with Hunt, too.

For the rest of the class, Katie watched the way Julie flirted with Hunt. Maybe she wasn't going to learn much Spanish today, but she was going to learn something!

When Katie got home that afternoon, she went into the kitchen and plunked her books on the counter.

Her brother was there, rooting around like a hungry weasel in the refrigerator.

"You're going to have to clear out on Saturday morning," Kevin said as he grabbed a huge apple and crunched down on it. "I don't want a walk-on type like you embarrassing a star like me by being around at my party."

Katie glared at her little brother and pushed past him. "This is my house, too!" she announced. "And I *will* hang around Saturday morning if I want to."

Kevin pulled the stem off his apple and flicked it at her. "You're jealous because I'm a TV star and you're not."

Katie felt the blood roar in her ears. Still, somehow she remained calm . . . at least on the outside. "You're not a star," she said coolly. "You're a dweeb who just happened to get lucky. When I get the lead in the school play, I'll be the one people notice."

With that, she turned and fled up the stairs, her bravado doing a crash and burn the minute she got into her room. She flopped on her bed and kicked off her sneakers. She'd probably goof up big time at the tryouts. But then she closed her eyes and thought of Hunt watching her as the lead in the play. She pictured him clapping wildly and jumping on stage to give her a bouquet of roses. It was such a delicious picture that she couldn't help feeling a little better.

Katie was quiet the next morning at school.

"What's with you?" Hilary asked.

Katie shrugged. "I was just thinking about what I should say to Hunt. It's the new, bold, go-after-what-I-want me."

Hilary paused and cocked her head. "Getting Hunt doesn't have anything to do with Kevin's winning all that stuff and being on TV, does it?"

Kate ignored the question. "Let's go to our lockers," she said. "Hunt will be walking by soon, and I want to be there."

At the lockers, Katie pretended to straighten her books while Hilary kept watch. After a while, Hilary whispered, "Don't look now. Your target is coming into sight."

Katie turned around and gave Hunt a dazzling smile.

"Oh, Hunt," she said, a little breathlessly. "Just the person I wanted to see."

"Uh, hi, Katie." Hunt raised one eyebrow and slowed down.

The green shirt Hunt was wearing made his eyes look even greener, Katie thought, feeling her throat close up. She stood there with an awkward expression on her face. She thought of Julie and how easy it was for her to flirt like mad. What would *she* do next?

"What's up?" Hunt asked quizzically.

Katie giggled the way she'd heard Julie giggle during class the day before. Then she tilted her head at precisely the same angle as Julie would have and asked, "Does something have to be up?"

"Well, no," he said, looking at her as though she had three heads. "I guess not."

Just then, Katie felt Hilary tug at her sweater sleeve. "Uh, we've gotta go," Hilary said.

"We've gotta go," Katie mimicked, as her friend practically pushed her past Hunt.

"Why'd you do that?" Katie hissed at Hilary when they had turned the corner. "I was trying to make conversation."

"Is that what you were doing?" asked Hilary. "It looked more like a stare-down."

"Look, it was your idea for me to flirt," Katie said angrily.

Hilary nodded. "Yeah, but you weren't flirting. You were putting on some kind of act."

Katie felt weird for a second. That's exactly how it had felt. But what else was she supposed to do—sit back and let the Julie Taylors of the world get all the guys? No way!

When Hunt walked into Spanish class, he glanced at Katie. Her heart jumped. Maybe she hadn't botched up this flirting thing after all. She smiled widely at him. He smiled back, but he turned around immediately and faced forward.

Julie Taylor leaned toward him. "Did you get the answer to number 10?" she asked.

He nodded, but didn't say anything more. A couple minutes later, Katie tapped him on the shoulder.

"Did you finish all the homework?" she asked in a sugary voice.

Hunt nodded slightly.

Katie giggled. "So did I," she said, but then she didn't have anything else to add. *Where does my brain go when I'm around him?* she wondered.

When the bell rang, she sprang from her chair and matched Hunt's stride to the front door.

"So, where are you going now?" she asked.

"To lunch like everybody else," he answered.

Katie rocked back on her heels. What a lame question she'd asked! She smiled weakly at Hunt, who had a blank look on his face. Then he suddenly said, "Hey, I heard about your brother."

Katie stepped back, surprised. Here she thought maybe she was getting Hunt to notice her, and he had to go and say something about her brother. "Oh, yeah," she managed.

"That's definitely cool," Hunt said, sounding enthusiastic for the first time.

"Yeah," Katie said dully. This conversation was going nowhere. She didn't want to talk about her stupid little brother.

But Hunt pressed on. "I heard he won some great stuff." Getting no response from Katie, he said, "Well, I gotta go. Some friends are saving me a place in the lunch line."

That night, Katie tried to figure out what she was doing wrong. She was flirting her head off, but Hunt wasn't reacting the way he was supposed to. She'd simply have to step up her efforts, she reasoned, trying to concentrate on her homework. If only flirting didn't feel so . . . fake.

The next morning, Katie took a long time dressing. She changed her outfit at least three times until she settled on a bright blue jacket and a multicolored blouse. Just for good measure she tied a long silk scarf around her neck. Then she put on her largest earrings and fussed with her hair, spraying it and fluffing it.

"You look weird," Kevin said, looking at her with bug eyes from the doorway. "You never used to be that bad of a dresser. And what did you do to your hair? Run it through Mom's pasta maker?"

"Shut up, Glop," Katie said, crashing past him as she heard a horn honk outside. "Or I'll run *you* through a pasta maker."

She ran outside and hopped into the car.

"Good morning," said Hilary's dad cheerfully from behind the wheel. He turned around to look at Katie, then he raised an eyebrow. "I didn't mean to rush you. You could have brushed your hair."

Hilary groaned. "Dad," she sputtered, then whispered to Katie, "Don't pay any attention to him."

Katie reached up and smoothed her hair. "Does it look bad?" Katie asked anxiously as they pulled away from the curb.

Hilary frowned. "Well, it's different. It's always hard when you try a new hairdo."

That wasn't what Katie wanted to hear. She craned her neck to see her reflection in the rearview mirror but gave up and slouched back in the seat. "Do you think this jacket and blouse are too bright together?"

Hilary smiled weakly and whispered, "No," but didn't elaborate.

"Good," Katie said. "Hunt can't fail to notice me today."

And sure enough Katie noticed immediately how Hunt stared at her when she walked into Spanish class. *This is really working,* she thought. She knew it was just a matter of time until Hunt found a private moment together to ask her out.

"I've been talking to Hunt and flirting like you said," Katie told her friend after class. "I think it's going to work. I just have to try harder."

"Well," Hilary said slowly, "Maybe you'd better back off for a while. Hunt doesn't seem to like girls who come on too strong."

Then she abruptly changed the subject. "Have you been studying for the audition?"

"Yeah," Katie answered. "I've read the script at least seventeen times. I've pretty much got my scene memorized. But we were talking about—"

"You're a great actress," Hilary interrupted. "Listen, I gotta go. I've got to take back a book I borrowed from Ms. Marsh."

Now what was that all about? Katie asked herself as Hilary hurried off.

♡ ♡ ♡

Monday morning at school, Katie hung around by her locker. No Hunt. He wasn't in Spanish class either, so Katie figured he must be out sick. But after lunch, she saw him walking quickly to his next class.

He didn't pass by her locker the next day, either. Katie began to wonder whether he was avoiding her, but she decided it wasn't worth getting paranoid until Spanish class. If he didn't show up there, something might really be wrong.

When she walked into Spanish class, Hunt wasn't there. Katie's heart sank. But just before the bell rang, he dashed in and quickly took his seat. When she tapped him on the shoulder, he shook her off as if she were a bug and didn't even turn around. Katie was hurt at first, but she figured he was just trying to put on a good show for the teacher. But when the dismissal bell rang, Hunt jumped up and bolted out the door.

"What do you suppose is going on with him?" Katie asked Hilary at lunch. "I've been acting like he's the center of the universe, and he's acting like he wishes I would fall off the planet."

Hilary shrugged and took a bite of her sandwich. "Who knows?" she said.

The next day, Katie resolved that she'd catch Hunt no matter how fast he tried to get away from her. Just before Spanish class, she headed for the restroom and piled on some more mascara. She frowned at her nails. Bor-ring! She'd go home tonight and paint them bright red. When she got to class, she wasn't surprised to see that Hunt wasn't there yet. Sure enough, just as the bell rang, he slid into his seat. *No problem*, Katie thought, waiting until the dismissal bell rang. When he got up, she'd be right on his heels. The bell rang, and he sprang up. She rushed out the door right behind him.

"Hunt, wait," she called.

He looked over his shoulder, then slowed and turned around to face her. She didn't mean to, but she heard herself giggle nervously.

Hunt flinched. "Katie, you know, I've been wanting to say something to you for a while," he said, then stopped himself as though he were having second thoughts.

Katie's heart seemed to turn completely over. This was it—he was going to ask her out.

"I don't know what's gotten into you, Katie," he said, almost harshly. Then he added, more softly, "You've changed."

Katie could hardly stand still. Finally he was admitting that he'd been noticing her! She waited to hear the boy of her dreams ask her out.

"The thing is," he went on. "I liked you better the way you were before."

Katie's eyes welled up with tears. She felt as though someone had slammed a soccer ball into her stomach. *What?* She opened her mouth to reply, but no words would come. She was finally able to stammer, "I . . . I have to meet a friend for lunch."

♡ ♡ ♡

"I never should have opened my mouth around him," she moaned to Hilary as they walked home from school that afternoon.

"Flirting is one thing," said Hilary gently. "But, Katie, you didn't have to take it so far."

"I made a total fool of myself," Katie said, tiredly. Then suddenly she got angry. "Why didn't you stop me? You're supposed to be my friend!"

"I tried to," Hilary said, a little hurt. "But you were acting like a real—"

"Flirt," said Katie, finishing her sentence. "Just like you told me to act."

Now it was Hilary's turn to get mad. "Listen, Katie, just because your little brother won some stupid prizes on 'The Glop Show' doesn't give you the right to—" She stopped herself and tried to calm down. "Look, you don't need to *act* like a flirt, you just need to be who you are and let Hunt get to know you. He was already noticing you a ton before you—"

"Before *you* made me blow it," Katie shouted, stomping off.

The rest of the way home, she felt like running back to her friend and apologizing. Why was she acting like such a jerk?

♡　♡　♡

The next morning, Katie could barely crawl out of bed. She'd hardly slept at all, and when she stared at the plate of eggs her dad had fixed for her she thought she might be sick.

"Nervous about the play tryouts today?" her dad asked.

Katie was just about to tell him that she had decided not to go to the tryouts when Kevin bopped into the kitchen.

Katie glared at him.

"What's your problem?" he asked. Then he said, "Oh I get it. Today's your big acting chance! Well, take it from me—if you've got what it takes, it's easy to be a star."

Her dad dropped a reassuring arm around Katie's shoulder. "All you have to do is try your best. That's what tryouts are all about—trying."

Katie looked at her dad helplessly. She didn't have the heart to tell him what a chicken she was.

Later, as Hilary's dad drove them to school, Katie looked over at her friend. Hilary was staring silently out the window.

"Will you go with me to the tryouts today?" Katie asked, softly. "You know, for moral support?"

Hilary turned away from the window and stared at Katie coldly, but then her face grew warm. "Does this mean the real Katie has returned?"

Katie smiled and nodded. "She sure has— except for when I go up in front of Mr. Finnerty and get that leading role. Then I'm going to do some *real* acting."

That afternoon at the tryouts, Katie remembered all but one of her lines. When she walked to the back of the room to sit with Hilary and watch the others who were trying out, Hilary gave her a thumbs-up sign and whispered "Good job!" in her ear.

Katie cringed a little as Julie Taylor stepped to the front of the classroom to audition next. As she watched Julie, Katie had to admit that she was pretty good. She would probably get the part, and she'd deserve it, too.

As Katie and Hilary got up to leave after everyone had auditioned, Katie stopped dead in her tracks. Hunt was standing in the doorway to the classroom. He'd probably seen the whole audition! At first Katie's heart did a back flip, but then she realized he'd probably come to watch Julie.

She grabbed Hilary's arm. "Hunt's here," she whispered frantically in her friend's ear. "Help me get past him without making a fool of myself again."

Hilary stepped in front of Katie. "Follow me," she said, walking toward the door.

"Wasn't she great?" Hunt asked, just as the two girls were about to pass him.

Who was he talking about? Katie wondered. She was sure it was Julie.

But just then Hunt stopped them both. "I didn't know you were such a good actress," he said to Katie, his green eyes dancing. "You sure were a lousy flirt."

Katie's face grew warm, and then she laughed.

Hilary smiled. "I've got to be going," she said, making a hasty exit.

Katie and Hunt barely noticed her leave. They were too busy staring into each other's eyes and acting as though they were falling in love.

Love Throws Her a Curve

"I think this is it!" Aubrey's big sister Melinda announced dramatically. She whirled around the room, then threw herself rather dramatically onto Aubrey's just-made bed. "This time, I am totally and completely in love."

Aubrey paused in mid-chew and set down her cinnamon toast. "Two things. You're lying on my favorite mitt, which I need for my game. And do you think I care the slightest bit that you're in love? Pu-leeze!"

Melinda glared at her. "Your uniform's dirty," she said, eyeing Aubrey's muddy white pants.

"So what?" Aubrey shot back.

Melinda rolled on her back and stared at the ceiling. "I'm totally in love with Brett Blackwell."

Aubrey snorted. "Oh, pu-leeze. I know his little brother, J.D. He's got the same hair, the same smile. He's tall. And oh, yeah: He's a pain. It must run in the family."

Melinda went on the attack. "You still think the whole world revolves around sports," she said with big-sister superiority. "Oh, well. I suppose I didn't know much about love when I was only in junior high."

Aubrey grabbed her glove. "Well I know the world sure doesn't revolve around you and Brett Blackwell." And with that Aubrey was out the door. She didn't have time to worry about her sister's latest love. Her softball game started in 15 minutes.

Thirteen minutes later, Aubrey dashed into the dugout. Her fellow Sassy Sluggers were psyched. "We've gotta get these guys," she whispered excitedly to Laurel Michaels, the catcher. "The Bat Busters are pretty good."

"Piece of cake," Laurel responded, trying to sound not the least bit concerned. She stopped and looked Aubrey up and down. "Boy, your uniform's dirty today."

Aubrey took off the baseball cap she loved, then smoothed her unruly hair back under it. "I know," she sighed. "I was practicing sliding all afternoon in my backyard."

"Well, I hope your pitching is on today," Laurel said, picking up her bat as she heard the umpire call Batter Up. "We've gotta win this game."

As Aubrey watched her friend walk out to the plate, she heard somebody call her name. *Oh, great. What's he doing here?* she thought, seeing J.D. Blackwell coming up to her. He was probably going to bug her again about defecting from the Sassy Sluggers in order to join his team, Harlan's Heating and Plumbing. He'd asked her at least sixteen times since their pitcher had broken his arm two weeks ago.

"I told you, I've made up my mind. I'm sticking with the Sluggers," she said before he even opened his mouth.

"Did I say a word?" J.D. said, with a lazy smile.

"So what do you want, then?" she said, squinting at the sun in her eyes.

J.D. pushed back a lock of dark hair that had fallen across his forehead. "Nothing. I just wanted to wish you luck. The Bat Busters are tough."

"Like I don't know that?" Aubrey said. She eyed J.D., taking in his tall, slim frame and intense green eyes. He actually wasn't *that* dorky looking.

J.D. gave her a thumbs-up sign and grinned. "Mind if I watch?"

"What?" She had been staring at the weird dimple in his chin. "Oh, yeah, right. Uh, sure. Stick around if you want."

Aubrey watched J.D. clamber up to the top of the grandstand. Great. Was he going to stay and watch the entire game? Didn't he have anything better to do on a Saturday afternoon?

♡ ♡ ♡

The excitement mounted as the game went into the third inning with the score 4–2, Sluggers in the lead. Aubrey was pitching better than ever—until J.D. started cheering for her. Then her windups started to go haywire and her next three pitches were met with resounding cracks of Bat Buster bats.

"Come on, Aubrey!" yelled J.D.

"Shut up, J.D.," Aubrey mumbled to herself. She tried to focus but her eyes kept straying to J.D. in the grandstand. Finally, after forbidding herself to look at him again, she started finding her pitching groove again.

By then, though, the Bat Busters had evened the score. Aubrey had to think of something fast. The Sluggers *had* to win this game.

The next few innings were very tense, and although the Sluggers started hitting well, the Bat Busters' defense was tough. It wasn't until the sixth inning that things started to go in the Sluggers' favor. Laurel slapped out a double. Then Aubrey stepped up and delivered a ball to left center that drove in Laurel's run. Finally, the Sassy Sluggers won, but by only one run.

The Sluggers went crazy in the dugout, laughing and hugging each other. Then they dumped a cooler of water on Coach McKelvy's head.

"Whew!" Laurel said, giving Aubrey a high five. "We almost didn't pull that one through. What happened to you out there?"

Aubrey shook her head. "I dunno," she said, not wanting to admit that J.D. had gotten to her. "My sister's bugging me big time."

Laurel smiled mischievously. "Oh, no. Don't tell me."

Aubrey nodded. Then they said in unison, "She's in love again!"

Laurel rolled her eyes. "Some girls just don't get it."

Aubrey agreed. "Yeah, tell me something I don't know." She picked up her equipment. "Want to come over?"

Laurel shook her head. "It's my grandmother's birthday."

Aubrey shrugged. "Well, call me tonight," she said, as her friend walked off. "I'll give you an update on Melinda's love story."

After accepting congratulations from the parents of the other players, Aubrey left the field for home. She hoped Melinda was there. Even if all she wanted to talk about was Brett, at least Aubrey would have someone to go out for frozen yogurt with.

"Hey, Aub." Aubrey didn't need to turn around to see who was calling her. She knew it was J.D.

"What?" she asked, continuing to walk on. She had no desire to talk to Public Enemy Number One. He'd almost caused her to lose the game, and his stupid brother was turning her sister into a lovesick moron. She'd had about enough of the Blackwell family.

"Congrats," J.D. said, breaking into a lope to catch up with her.

Aubrey felt as though she were brushing aside a pesky fly. "Yeah, no thanks to you! Your yelling at me made me lose my concentration."

73

"Hey!" J.D. sounded hurt. "I was just cheering you on. I didn't mean to throw you off."

Aubrey shrugged. Maybe it wasn't his fault. Maybe she'd just had trouble focusing. She smiled at him. "That's okay," she said, deciding that now that he was walking with her, it beat walking alone.

"My brother likes your sister," J.D. said suddenly. "I know because I saw him looking at her picture in the yearbook."

"Dumb, huh?" Aubrey said, wondering why it didn't look like J.D. was as bothered about it as she was. "Isn't Brett acting weird? Melinda sure is."

J.D. chuckled. "He's acting as if Melinda's some kind of goddess."

Aubrey pretended to fluff up her hair like a beauty queen and they both burst out laughing. Then they fell into an awkward silence.

As they crossed the street in front of Aubrey's house, J.D. finally said something. "So, have you given any more thought to joining my team? We could use your good batting. You have the best hitting average around."

Aubrey sighed. So that was the real reason J.D. had followed her home. To bug her again about quitting the Sluggers and joining his team. She was an idiot to have started enjoying herself in any way, shape, or form.

"I've *told* you already—I like my team. I like my friends—" She stopped. J.D. wasn't even looking at her. She followed his eyes to her front porch where Brett and Melinda were giving each other longing looks.

"Don't they make you sick?" Aubrey hissed at J.D.

"What?" J.D. mumbled. "They're just talking. Lots of people do that."

"Let's get out of here," Aubrey said, spinning on her heels.

"Right behind you," J.D. replied, fumbling in his pockets. He pulled out a five dollar bill. "I've got enough money to buy us each a frozen yogurt."

Aubrey regarded J.D. for a moment. "Frozen yogurt sounds good, but I can buy my own." She dug into her pockets, but came up with only two dimes.

J.D. looked at the two coins. "Like I said, I'll treat."

Their eyes locked for a moment. Neither wanted to give an inch.

"I was the one who suggested it," J.D. said evenly. "I'll pay."

Aubrey gave up. "Fine," she said, handing him the dimes. "This will buy my topping." She paused for a minute and looked at her muddy uniform. "I guess I'm pretty dirty though," she muttered, suddenly embarrassed.

J.D. nodded. "So what? I think you look fine."

Before she knew it, Aubrey found herself sitting across from J.D. at Abernathy's Yogurt Shop and having a pretty good time. J.D. had ordered the most disgusting combination: banana and blueberry

yogurt combined, topped with Oreo cookies, and it was all Aubrey could do to eat her peach yogurt without laughing at the funny faces he was making.

After a while, the conversation got serious when J.D. started asking Aubrey about how he could get more of a spin on his fastball. They talked about other teams and exchanged batting tips, too. By the time they got up to leave, Aubrey decided that J.D. was an okay guy, even though she knew that he was just being nice to convince her to join his team.

"I still can't believe what total nerds Melinda and your brother are being," Aubrey said as they neared her house. "I hope they're not still there."

J.D. shot her a look. "People can't help it if they like each other."

Aubrey shot him a look back. "Well, people shouldn't waste their time," she said defensively. "For one thing, it messes up their concentration."

Aubrey waited for a reply, but there was none, and J.D. walked without saying a word the whole way home. When they got to the foot of her driveway she thanked him for the yogurt, hoping he would say something to her. But J.D. just mumbled, "You're welcome," and took off.

"What's he all tweaked about?" Aubrey grumbled, watching him go.

Later, talking to Laurel on the phone, Aubrey made fun of Melinda and Brett, but she didn't mention that she had gone to get yogurt with J.D.

She didn't know why she "forgot" to tell her friend since she never kept anything from Laurel. But somehow, this seemed . . . well, private.

After she hung up the phone, Aubrey headed down to the family room, where Melinda was watching a rock video. "You and J.D. were walking awfully close together," Melinda said, wriggling her eyebrows up and down. "But I have news for you, baby sister: You're too much of a jock for love. Guys go for girls who act at least halfway feminine."

"Lay off," Aubrey snapped, as she sprawled on the couch.

Suddenly, she found herself thinking about how quiet J.D. had gotten on the way home. "You and Brett sure looked ridiculous giggling together," she said, trying to concentrate on irritating her sister.

Melinda slouched deeper into her seat. "For your information, Brett and I were talking about *important* things. Brett's very smart. Did you know he's president of the sophomore class?"

"Big, hairy deal."

Melinda glared at Aubrey, then turned back to the video.

For a while, Aubrey tried to concentrate on the video, but she couldn't stop thinking about J.D. If only she knew something about guys. But who could she ask? Laurel didn't know anything. None of her friends did. Finally, desperation took over and she decided Melinda was her only choice.

"Mel, can I ask you a question?"

Melinda shook her head, but Aubrey persisted. "Have you ever kind of liked being around someone, but most of the time that person bugged you to join their team? And then when you didn't join that person got all mad?"

Melinda looked like she was trying not to smile. "J.D.'s really getting to you, huh?"

"Oh, never mind," Aubrey said, quickly leaving the room.

♡ ♡ ♡

Monday morning at school, Aubrey had just left the cafeteria with her juice and a bag of chips when she spotted J.D. going up to Ann Stauffer. Ann was cute and bubbly. Worse, she was the shortstop for the Bat Busters. Aubrey watched as something J.D. said made Ann laugh so hard that she threw back her glossy blond hair. Aubrey turned away. And when J.D. ran up behind her, calling her name, she just kept walking as though she didn't hear him.

"What's your problem?" J.D. said, stepping in front of her.

"I don't want to be on your team," Aubrey said sharply.

J.D. shrugged. "I know. I told you yesterday that I understood."

"Well, you sure didn't waste any time going after Ann Stauffer."

J.D. looked puzzled. "So why are you mad? You've only told me about eight million times you don't want to join my team."

Aubrey knew that was true. Why *was* she so mad? She stood there like an idiot, and finally J.D. just shrugged and walked off.

Confused, Aubrey sat on a bench to eat her chips, when Laurel came up and sat next to her. "I heard you talking with J.D.," Laurel said, munching on her cookie. "Why are you so mean to him? He's been so nice to you—and he's kind of cute, in case you haven't noticed."

Aubrey looked at her friend. "I wasn't mean." She considered it for a minute. "Well, maybe I was hard on him. But he's such a pain."

After school, Aubrey went straight to her room to do her homework, willing to do anything to get J.D. off her mind. As she started to get into it, Melinda walked in and flopped down on her rug.

"Brett just called," she said, hugging herself.

For some reason, Aubrey burst into tears.

"Aub, what's wrong?" Melinda said with real concern in her eyes.

Soon Aubrey found herself telling Melinda everything. About how J.D. used to bug her to join his team. About how he was now asking Ann instead. About his strange silence after a pretty nice afternoon at the yogurt shop.

"He's a total pain, so why do I feel so bad?" she sobbed.

Melinda looked at Aubrey thoughtfully. "It's simple. He likes you. You like him. I thought you were too hooked on sports to fall in love, but I think love has thrown you a curve."

Aubrey was about to yell indignantly that there was no way she was falling for J.D., but something stopped her. Maybe it was okay to admit she liked him a little. As long as it didn't throw off her concentration. "But why J.D.?" she asked softly. "I know lots of guys at school who are better looking—and who have better batting averages."

"Love is weird," Melinda said simply. "You'll figure it out."

"Well, I'd better figure it out before Thursday night. That's when we play the Fire Belles. My concentration has to be totally on. If we win that game, we'll be in the city play-offs!"

♡   ♡   ♡

Thursday night, Aubrey put on her uniform—clean this time—and tried to stay focused. She even went to the field early to get her head into the game. As she stood on the pitcher's mound ready to pitch to an imaginary batter, J.D. walked onto the field and went up to the plate.

"Want to throw a few?" he said, nonchalantly. "I'll be your catcher."

Aubrey stood frozen on the mound. For some reason, she felt totally shy, a feeling she'd never felt around J.D. before. She didn't know what to say, then suddenly, she blurted out, "So, did Ann Stauffer turn you down? Is that why you're here? To seriously annoy me again?"

"No," he said, coolly. "Ann said yes."

Aubrey thought about that for a second. "And you're still coming around to help me with my pitching?"

J.D. nodded. "That's right."

"Why?" Aubrey demanded, narrowing her eyes.

J.D. just looked at her and smiled. "Come on, burn one in," he said, slapping his mitt.

Aubrey thought about the way he was looking at her. Suddenly, the realization hit her: J.D. *liked* her, and what's more, *she* liked him. A lot. Like the way Melinda liked Brett. And now it was okay to admit it not only to herself, but to J.D. as well.

She drew back for her windup. "My batting average is better than Ann's."

J.D. laughed. "I know. Be quiet and pitch. I promise, I won't disturb your concentration. Besides, if you win, you're taking *me* out for frozen yogurt."

"You're on," Aubrey said, pitching a real winner.

Lost: One Boyfriend

THWAK!

A note in the shape of a football landed on Caitlin's desk. She glanced up quickly to see whether Mr. Davidson, her science teacher, had noticed.

He was writing some weird theory on the board, so Caitlin quickly unfolded the note. She was sure it was sent by her best friend, Tamara, who was sitting two rows behind her.

Guess what? Tamara had written in her big, loopy handwriting. *That new guy in English class called me last night! Meet me at the library after school today, and we can work together. Tam*

P.S. Mr. Davidson has bug eyes and gives us too much homework—it's the pits!

Caitlin tore out a piece of notebook paper to reply. But then she heard Mr. Davidson's booming voice directed right at her.

"Do you agree with Mr. Jennings, Miss Martin?"

Caitlin ducked her head. If she agreed, she'd have to explain why. If she disagreed, she'd have to say what she thought. She was doomed!

Mr. Davidson narrowed his eyes behind his thick glasses when he saw Caitlin's mouth drop open. "Paying attention might help, Miss Martin."

Caitlin mumbled an apology as Evan Barnes raised his hand and said in an obnoxious tone, "I agree with Mr. Jennings."

"I agree with Mr. Jennings," Caitlin mimicked under her breath. She and Evan had had a competitive thing going for the last couple of years. *Just look at him,* she thought. *What a goofy smile! How could all the girls in eighth grade be bonkers over him?*

Turning back to more important matters, Caitlin slipped the note from Tamara into her book. As soon as Mr. Davidson turned his back to put away some disgusting creature preserved in formaldehyde, she scribbled a note to Tamara: *Meet you at the library after school. C.*

She folded it up, took aim, and started to flip it to Tamara. But just as she let it fly, she sneezed, and the note flopped onto Evan Barnes's desk.

As he read the note, Evan's dark brown eyes crinkled up at the sides. Then he looked Caitlin's way and flashed her an 80-megawatt smile.

Caitlin's cheeks went on fire. He thought she wanted to meet *him* at the library! Well, she'd have to set him straight the second class ended.

When the bell sounded, she quickly strode over to Evan's desk. "Listen, creep—" she began, but her sentence was cut off as "Turbo Mouth" Linda

swooped in on Evan and started talking to him at the speed of light.

"Evan," gushed Linda. "Can you come to the recycling meeting after school today? We're trying to plan a big drive, and we need your ideas."

Evan shoved his hands in his pockets and nodded casually toward Caitlin. "Can't. I have to meet someone at the library after school."

Linda glanced at Caitlin and croaked, "Oh." Then she gathered up her books and walked hurriedly out of the classroom.

For the second time that day, Caitlin felt her cheeks glowing like molten lava. She glared at Evan, who didn't look even the least bit concerned. Didn't he know that Turbo Mouth wouldn't waste a minute blabbing to the whole school all kinds of rumors about them?

"Evan!" she burst out. "That note wasn't for you, and you know it!"

Evan just stood there, looking at Caitlin with the doofiest smile.

He's so conceited, she thought. *He still thinks I'm going to meet him at the library!*

"I wouldn't meet you at the library—or anywhere—even if you were the last person on earth!" she practically yelled at him.

Evan's face dropped for an instant, and Caitlin felt like she'd stepped on a puppy. The laughter was gone from Evan's eyes, replaced by a look Caitlin couldn't read.

"Hey, relax," he said in a quiet voice. "I knew the note wasn't meant for me. I was just kidding."

Feeling pretty horrible, Caitlin fled to meet Tamara, who was waiting at the door. "Quick!" Caitlin said. "Let's get out of here." She grabbed Tamara by the sleeve and started walking. It wasn't until they reached their lockers that she told her friend what had happened.

"It was such a rotten thing to say," Caitlin said. "Why was I so mean?"

"Well, you blew your chances with him," Tamara said, patting her friend's shoulder. "You're never going to get a guy that way."

Caitlin opened her locker and shoved her books in as if it were their fault that all this had happened. "I don't want to 'get' any guy," she said. "Just because *you're* guy crazy, Tamara, doesn't mean *I* am. Besides, I've got more important things to think about than guys. Especially guys like Evan Barnes."

"And what's wrong with Evan?" Tamara asked. "He's one of the cutest guys in school and it's obvious he likes you."

"He's conceited, for starters," Caitlin said, feeling herself getting really annoyed.

"He's self-confident!" Tamara shot back.

"He's a total flirt!" Caitlin said.

"He's social!" Tamara countered.

"He's a smart-aleck!" Caitlin said.

"He's got a sense of humor," retorted Tamara.

"And you have a serious sense of humor *failure* these days."

The bell rang and Caitlin slammed her locker shut. The girls glared at each other for a moment, then started to laugh. They set a time to meet in the study room at the library after school, and Caitlin headed off for P.E.

All during her warm-up exercises, Caitlin thought about Evan and about what Tamara had said. She wasn't used to the idea of a boy liking her. And Evan Barnes—why would a popular boy like him be interested in her? She was the quiet type, which he definitely was not. He was tall and kind of cute; and she was short and blah—not the kind of girl guys usually noticed. But could Tamara be right? Did Evan really like her? Sure, he looked at her a lot during science class. And he had asked her to be his lab partner once or twice. But she'd always figured it was because they were both good students. Still, Evan was—*oof!* Just then the soccer ball smacked into Caitlin's stomach.

"Get with the program!" Ms. Ladenheim yelled, blowing her whistle.

♡ ♡ ♡

Caitlin didn't think about Evan the rest of the day. In fact, she didn't think about him at all until he walked into science class the next day wearing a chocolate-brown shirt that made his blond hair look even blonder. Okay. So he wasn't *kinda* cute; he was *definitely* cute.

Mr. Davidson had brought in a desert tortoise for the class to study. Caitlin watched while Evan scratched the tortoise under its chin. The tortoise half-closed its eyes and appeared to be enjoying the scratching. Okay, so Evan was kind and gentle to animals. Big deal.

When it was her turn to observe the tortoise, Caitlin scratched the tortoise the way she'd seen Evan do it. She smiled shyly at Evan when he sat down. But he just looked through her and didn't smile back.

Caitlin went up to Tamara immediately after class. "I didn't apologize to Evan, but I smiled at him," she reported.

"That's a start," Tamara said. "By the way, that new guy in my English class asked me to go with him to the recycling club meeting next week."

Caitlin tried to act interested in her best friend's guy success, but inside she was wondering whether she really *had* blown it with Evan.

Over the next few days Caitlin realized that she was constantly on the lookout for Evan. She'd never looked for him before, and suddenly she was seeing him everywhere—walking down the halls between classes, talking with kids out by the front lawn before and after school, playing pickup basketball on the blacktop. She and Tamara usually sat on the library steps to eat lunch, but now she found herself persuading Tamara to move closer to the lunch benches where he sat. What was happening to her? She actually wanted to watch him *eat!* It was all too strange.

The next day, Mr. Davidson asked the science class to pick partners for a lab experiment. Caitlin gathered her courage and turned to Evan. "Do you want to be partners?" she asked.

Evan shrugged. "Whatever."

Stung, Caitlin turned away.

Later, when they were working on their amoeba project together, she tried to get him to talk to her, but he wouldn't say a single nonamoeba-related thing the whole time.

"You're right," she said mournfully to Tamara after school. "I blew it. Evan won't even speak to me, except to talk about lower life-forms."

Tamara patted her on the shoulder sympathetically. "Oh, well. We'll just find you another guy." She grinned suddenly. "I've got it! We'll put an ad in the school newspaper. Wanted: One boyfriend for Caitlin Martin."

Caitlin shoved her friend playfully. "You seem to be forgetting something: I'm not looking for a boyfriend!" She thought to herself, *I just want Evan.*

In her room after dinner, Caitlin started thinking about Tamara's totally zoided-out idea. Maybe she *should* put an ad in the paper, but instead it would read, "Lost: One boyfriend. Girl wants him back. Reward."

Then she told herself the whole idea was totally ridiculous. How could she lose a boyfriend when she never really had one in the first place? She decided to get some advice from her older brother, Albert—after all, he was a guy himself, wasn't he?

"Hey, Al," Caitlin said, walking into Albert's filthy room and plopping herself on his bed. "Let's say—let's just suppose—I kinda, you know, liked this guy, and—"

"Oh, I get it. You're in love," Albert said. "And you want to know how to make him like you, right?"

Caitlin bobbed her head up and down.

"Wear cute clothes," Albert said simply, trying to look very wise. "Guys like that." Then he broke into a mischievous smile. "And if you want to really get his attention, get good seats to a basketball game and ask him out."

Just then, their dad appeared in the doorway. "What's going on in here?" he asked.

"Nothing," Albert said, giving their dad an everything's-under-control look. "Caitlin and I are just talking."

When their dad left, Caitlin gave Albert a kiss on the cheek. All of her friends complained about their older brothers, she thought, leaving his room, but she sure got lucky.

The next day, Caitlin took extra care when she got dressed for school. She put on a pretty blue sweater that Tamara once told her made her eyes light up, and she selected just the right pair of earrings. Then she slipped into her mom's bathroom and sprayed a huge cloud of hair spray on her hair.

"Choke! Help! Toxic waste!" yelled Karen, her bratty little sister, poking her head in the doorway and grabbing her throat. "You'll asphyxiate the poor guy!"

"Lay off," Caitlin warned. Oh, well. At least she had one humanoid sibling in the family.

♡ ♡ ♡

Caitlin waited until just before the bell rang for science class so she could walk in when everyone was seated. She wanted Evan to notice her. She wanted him to see her in her blue sweater with her hair looking so good.

But when she got to her desk, she saw that Evan had his back to her. He was talking to a girl she didn't recognize.

"Good afternoon, class," said Mr. Davidson. "Before we begin with our paramecium project, I have an announcement. We have a new student here today. Her name is Nancy Powers. Please make her feel welcome."

Caitlin looked over to see a tall, confident girl with long, glossy hair that rippled down her back. She was wearing a dark red sweater and had long fingernails painted to match. Evan seemed totally ready to make her feel welcome, Caitlin noticed. In

92

fact, he helped Nancy during the entire class, and he walked her out when the bell rang.

"Nancy Powers has Evan all wrapped up, doesn't she?" Tamara announced as she and Caitlin walked down the hall.

Caitlin nodded miserably. *Lost: One boyfriend,* she thought.

"Too bad. Evan really liked you until you pounded on him," Tamara rambled on.

"Do you think I care?" Caitlin snapped.

Tamara blinked. "Sorry. I didn't realize you *did* care that much."

Caitlin shrugged. "I'm sorry. I just don't understand guys, that's all."

"Boys can be weird sometimes," Tamara said.

Right then and there Caitlin made up her mind to strike boys off her list forever. They were too much heartache. Instead, she would just throw herself into her schoolwork even harder. If she couldn't have Evan as her boyfriend, at least she would outshine him in class. In fact, for her next science report, she'd write something absolutely brilliant!

But even though she got an A on her report and Mr. Davidson read it aloud to the class, Evan didn't seem to care. All he seemed to care about was Nancy Powers—at least that's who he was staring at all during class.

It was all getting to be too much for Caitlin. She couldn't decide whether she was sad or just crazy. When the final bell of the day rang, Caitlin was totally depressed. And she couldn't even talk it over with Tamara, who had left early for a doctor's appointment.

Caitlin got her books out of her locker, walked to the front lawn, and slumped against a tree. She sat there for a while watching kids laughing and jostling each other as they waited for the bus to pick them up.

Suddenly, a note landed in front of her on the grass.

"Go ahead, open it. It's for you," said a male voice.

Caitlin looked up to see Evan towering over her.

"Great report you did in Davidson's class."

"Yeah, right. Like you heard a word of it."

"Oh, come on," he said. "Lighten up. You're sorry, I'm sorry. Let's just forget it and be friends." He smiled and sat down on the grass beside her.

Caitlin took a relieved breath. "I guess I should have said I was sorry sooner," she said at last.

Evan picked a blade of grass and tied it in a knot. "Whatever. But when I heard your report, I got to thinking. Maybe you can't take it when someone teases you, but you're still smart and fun . . . and you're just as pretty as Nancy."

Evan was actually telling her he liked her! She'd won him back. *Found: One boyfriend!*

"Go ahead," Evan said, pointing to the note. "Open it."

Caitlin unfolded the note and read, *Come with me to the library—and then afterward, we'll go for a soda.*

On the back of the note Evan had written her name with his . . . inside a big heart!

Heads Up for Love

"Heads up!" Casey's voice rang down the barn aisle at Rolling Meadows Riding Club. She poked her head between the stall bars, her black bangs matted down where her velvet hunt cap had been.

"Ask me if I care," Alexandra muttered, recognizing her boy-crazy friend's code signaling that a cute guy was nearby. She turned toward the gate to see Brian Donnelly climbing out of his dad's fancy sports car.

"Well, maybe you should start caring," Casey replied. "Some of the guys at school think you're cute, but they're starting to think you've gone over the edge with this horse stuff. I mean, I like horses, too, but ever since you got this job you're practically turning *into* a horse."

Alexandra neighed at her friend. "You know," she said sarcastically, "you might be right."

Casey rolled her eyes and walked away. "I'm just being a good friend," she said over her shoulder.

Alexandra started brushing Pride's glossy, bay coat with renewed vigor. The gentle mare turned her head and looked at Alexandra questioningly with liquid brown eyes. Alexandra sighed and patted Pride's velvety muzzle.

"Sorry, girl. I guess I was brushing a little hard." She set the currycomb on the shelf and put her arms around Pride's strong neck. "It's just that whenever any guy shows up here at the barn, Casey gets terminally weird." Alexandra picked up the comb and resumed brushing Pride's coat, more softly this time.

"It's totally ridiculous," she went on, oblivious to the fact that Pride was paying no attention and had shoved her nose into her manger, searching for any remaining hay. "All the boys around here ride like nerds, anyway."

Pride snorted and shook her head.

"Okay," Alexandra said with a laugh. "You're right. Brian Donnelly can ride, but he doesn't count because he knows how good he is, and he won't let anyone forget it. I'm sure glad that he's not in any of my classes. I'd make him ride without stirrups until he was so sore he couldn't walk!"

As she tossed her thick, strawberry-blond braid out of the way, she caught a glimpse of the clock on the wall. Oops—it was almost 4:30. She'd better get out to the ring, pronto. She was scheduled to teach a lesson, and the head riding instructor, Janine Cochran, wouldn't like it if she were late. Alexandra knew that she'd been lucky to get the job as student assistant, and she'd almost blown it by daydreaming once before. She rushed over to the tack room for

Pride's saddle and bridle, and she had the mare ready to go in minutes.

As she rode toward the ring, Alexandra saw Brian. He was waiting for a groom to hand him the reins for his horse, Sinbad, a huge gelding that was as black as coal. Alexandra shook her head. Brian was so spoiled. As far as she was concerned, the only thing he had going for him was his horse. She was just entering the ring when she heard Sinbad trotting up behind her.

"Alexandra, wait," Brian called.

Alexandra froze. The whole time she'd been riding at Rolling Meadows, Brian had never lowered himself to talk to her. What could he want now?

"You're Janine's assistant, right?" he asked.

Alexandra nodded, her hands gripping Pride's reins tighter. If he dared to ask her to go fetch his gloves or something, she'd let him know exactly what she thought of him.

"Listen," he said, checking her over with a cool look in his icy-blue eyes. "My cousin's here for the summer. He's never been near a horse in his life, and he's decided he wants to ride." This last sentence came out like a sneer. "He's basically a case. Kicked out of at least a couple of schools. My dad says his next stop will probably be one of those schools for total derelicts. I'm supposed to be a good influence on him."

Well, you'll be an influence, anyway, Alexandra thought to herself. She tried not to let her disgust register in her face. It wasn't smart to upset good customers, not if she wanted to keep her job.

"What's this got to do with me?" she asked, guardedly.

Brian shrugged and flicked his riding crop against his tall, black hunt boots. "Janine said you teach the beginners, so I guess that means you'll be teaching my cousin. His name's Trent."

For a second, Alexandra found herself feeling sorry for Trent, whoever he was. Imagine being related to Brian!

"Well, anyway, don't let him embarrass me any more than he has to. Babysit him, will you?"

Alexandra set her jaw. "No problem," she heard herself say in a tight voice that didn't sound anything like her own.

Brian mumbled a thank-you, then dug his heels into Sinbad's sides. The big horse jerked forward, and Alexandra had to look away so she wouldn't have to witness any more of Brian's carelessness. Poor Sinbad, she thought. Such a great horse, stuck with such a loser of an owner.

"Alexandra!"

It was Janine, calling from her director's chair at the side of the ring. When Alexandra reached her, Janine was just standing up to greet a tall, serious boy who was awkwardly plodding into the ring on an old, gray gelding.

Alexandra squinted in the bright afternoon sun. She didn't recognize the rider, but she knew poor Midnight. He was a sour old horse who'd been a champion a long time ago and had been more or less retired for a few years. He was only ridden when no other horse was available.

"Alexandra," Janine said in her businesslike voice, "this is Trent Merrick, Brian Donnelly's cousin. Trent will be riding with us this summer, and you'll be his instructor." Janine paused, looking Alexandra squarely in the face. "He wants to get ready for the Labor Day horse show."

Alexandra almost snorted, but she didn't dare —not when faced with Janine's steely gaze. She gave Trent a long look. He was kind of cute, in that same surfer-blond way that Brian was. But where Brian looked like a self-confident jerk, Trent looked just plain tough. His hair was longer than that of any of the boys at her school. And his eyes, hard and blue, looked as though they could cut right through a person. Still, no tough-guy act could keep him from looking pretty funny up on a horse. Alexandra wanted to choke back a laugh. He was sitting all wrong in Midnight's saddle, and his elbows stuck out like wings.

"Make a rider of him," Janine said in a tone that Alexandra knew well. It meant, *Do it even if it's impossible.*

"No problem," Alexandra said forcefully, more to convince herself than anyone else. Was this Janine's idea of a test to see whether she could cut it? Alexandra felt a rush of anger toward Trent. Was this guy who looked like a street fighter going to make her look like a total fool? Not if she had anything to do with it, she decided.

"Let's go," she said sharply, motioning to Trent with her riding crop.

She nudged Pride forward and was surprised to hear Midnight trotting behind her. The stubborn horse was well known for planting his hooves and not moving for anyone or anything. Alexandra hoped Trent wasn't following his cousin's bad example and wearing sharp spurs. Influence—yeah, right!

Alexandra turned around and watched as Trent flopped around impossibly on Midnight's bony back. No, no spurs. Just worn-out western boots that somehow looked right on him, even if he should have been wearing totally different boots with an English saddle.

When they got to the far corner of the ring, Alexandra reined Pride in and turned to Trent. "I think we'll start with a few basics," she said. "But I'll cut the lesson short so you won't get too tired."

"I came here to ride," Trent said sharply. "Don't go easy on me."

"Okay. Let's start with the horse," Alexandra said flatly. "First lesson, find another one. Midnight is bad news. He doesn't like to do anything anyone tells him, and I heard he's thrown more people than anyone can count."

"I like Midnight," Trent said simply, as if the matter were settled. "I liked him the minute I saw him pawing the dirt in the paddock by the front gate. We understand each other."

Alexandra shook her head. Trent just didn't get it. "Now, about those elbows . . ." she began, sighing. She sure had her work cut out for her.

Later that afternoon, as Alexandra cooled her mare off after Trent's lesson, she looked over by the north barn, where Trent was leading Midnight toward his stall. Midnight's head was cocked in a funny way right toward Trent's ear. If Alexandra didn't know better, she'd swear that the old horse and Trent were talking to each other. She took off her hunt cap and shook out her hair. Ridiculous. Then, as if Trent could sense she was watching him, he suddenly turned around and flashed her a smile.

"He's as conceited as his cousin!" Alexandra said aloud, turning away quickly, her cheeks strangely warm. "C'mon, Pride. It's time to put you away."

Just then, Casey came up behind Alexandra and fell into step with her. "You poor thing. Brian told me that you were stuck with his juvenile delinquent cousin. Why does he ride with his elbows sticking out like that?"

Alexandra glanced over her shoulder and saw Trent gently placing a blanket on Midnight. Then she looked over at Sinbad, whom the groom had just finished blanketing. Brian was probably sitting in his dad's fancy car, waiting impatiently for Trent to finish up. Well, Trent wasn't about to hurry when it came to Midnight. Alexandra smiled. *Good for you, Trent,* she thought, in spite of her annoyance at his cool exterior.

"Trent's not such a bad rider," she said to Casey. "Another lesson or two and he won't stick his elbows out anymore. You'll see."

"Brian told me that Trent is bad news," Casey said. "He's staying with Brian's family so he won't be around his bad-guy buddies in the city."

Alexandra just shrugged. It probably was better for Trent to hang out with Midnight than those buddies of his. She put Pride away and tried to forget about the rough guy she was supposed to turn into a polished rider by the time the Labor Day horse show rolled around. But how could she forget about him? He might make her lose her job if she didn't get him into shape!

♡ ♡ ♡

Two days later, Alexandra saddled up and headed toward the ring, where three of her favorite beginning riders were waiting eagerly on their ponies. Alexandra smiled and nudged Pride with her legs. After teaching Mr. Cool, it would be nice to work with three pony-crazy little girls.

As she rode closer, Alexandra saw Janine jerk her chin to the far corner of the ring, where Trent was trotting around on Midnight. "Trent wants you to teach him," Janine said. "I'll take the girls today."

Alexandra managed to nod, and hide her disappointment. As she rode up to Trent, Midnight pinned back his ears and stretched his neck out to bite Pride, but Alexandra spun Pride sharply out of the way just in time.

"I thought I told you to choose another horse," she practically snarled at Trent. "I don't want him taking a hunk out of mine."

Trent regarded her, lifting one eyebrow lazily. "Midnight didn't mean it. Did you, boy?" He gave the old horse a gentle pat. "Besides, I told you, Midnight and I understand each other."

"And I thought you wanted to learn to ride," Alexandra snapped. "That horse is old and mean. No one could possibly look good riding him."

Trent looked contemptuously at Alexandra. "My uncle told me that no one is a true horseman unless he can make *any* horse look good—not just the good-looking ones." He flashed a grin. "That would include Midnight."

Alexandra felt her cheeks heat up. "Well, uh, yeah," she stammered. And Trent was right. In fact, he'd just about stated Rule Number Two of horsemanship, which came right after Rule Number One: Love your horse.

Trent patted Midnight firmly on his neck. He saw that he had stumped her and was acting extra cool about it. "Whatcha staring at?" he asked, nonchalantly. "Teach me to ride." He pulled his elbows in and trotted off.

"Heels down," Alexandra commanded, searching for something else that Trent was doing wrong. "Back straight!"

"Okay, Teach," Trent said, grinning at her with his impossible grin that made her want to ride away and never look back. But Alexandra needed this job. So she barked out orders instead. She'd turn this juvenile delinquent into a rider if it killed her.

"You'll never get him to slow down if you don't communicate what you want," Alexandra said to Trent, who was already galloping by the end of the lesson and was almost out of control. "I said canter, not gallop! Close your hands on the reins."

"I thought you said this old horse wouldn't move!" Trent said, pulling up in front of Alexandra.

Alexandra didn't have an answer. What was it about this guy who couldn't ride worth beans that made Midnight respond to him? Still, Trent did have a *way* about him . . . a way with horses, anyway. If only he weren't so arrogant! It must run in the family, she thought, thinking of Brian.

"So what do you think?" Trent asked. "Are we ready for the show—I mean Midnight and I?"

"You've got a lot to learn before Labor Day," Alexandra said.

"That just means you've got a lot to teach," Trent replied. "Think you can handle it?"

"Oh, spare me. You're not the first rider to come around here with an attitude. Don't think you're so special."

Alexandra clapped her hand over her mouth. She'd been rude to a Rolling Meadows customer. What would Janine say? She'd probably toss her off the property the minute she found out!

Trent only smiled. "Don't worry about it, tough girl. I won't squeal on you. Besides, I can tell you're just talk." He laughed. "You know something? You and Midnight are a lot alike."

What was that supposed to mean? Alexandra wondered. But aloud she said, "And you're not as tough as you think you are. I've seen you whisper sweet nothings into that horse's ear."

Trent's blue eyes sparkled. "You're on to me. Don't let anyone in on my secret. They think I'm trouble—I guess I kind of like it that way."

♡ ♡ ♡

The next few lessons went by smoothly. As the Labor Day horse show approached, Alexandra had to admit that tough-guy Trent might even make a decent rider. He and Midnight were forming a pretty solid partnership, and Alexandra found herself actually looking forward to working with both of them.

One day, after a particularly good lesson, Trent suggested that they cool their horses down by walking up the trail. The two rode companionably side by side, hardly talking, just enjoying the scenery around them.

"Only a few more weeks until the horse show," Trent said suddenly.

Alexandra felt something catch in her throat. Only a few more weeks and Trent would be heading back to the city. She wouldn't be teaching him anymore. She heard herself make a funny choking noise.

"What was that sound supposed to mean?" Trent's eyes narrowed and flashed dangerously. "You don't think I can do it, do you?"

Alexandra shook her head. "No, I didn't say that," she said quickly.

"Brian doesn't think I can do it either. He makes fun of Midnight and brays like a donkey whenever I talk about him."

Alexandra nearly exploded. "You might not have been riding for long, but you're more of a horseman than he'll ever be!"

Trent's eyes met hers. "Thank you for saying that," he said. "That means more to me than any blue ribbon ever could."

Alexandra thought about Brian spurring Sinbad, and about his tossing the horse's reins to a groom. She'd never seen him comb his own horse or tuck him into his stall for the night. "You're going to rub your blue ribbon right in Brian's face!" she said, determined to make sure that happened.

For the next few weeks, Alexandra didn't allow herself to think about the fact that Trent would be leaving soon. She wondered why that was on her mind, anyway. It was her job to concentrate solely on his riding and on strengthening his partnership with Midnight. She had to admit that he was doing a pretty good job on that last part himself. All anyone had to do was look at Midnight. The old horse's shabby coat practically gleamed now and his eyes were bright in a way that Janine said she hadn't seen since Midnight had torn up the horse show circuit a few years ago. Trent just might be able to pull off the Labor Day horse show after all, Alexandra thought.

♡ ♡ ♡

"Are you crazy?" Casey asked when Alexandra told her one afternoon that she thought Trent would cinch the blue ribbon at the horse show.

Alexandra thought of Trent and Midnight and smiled. "Maybe I am," she said, thinking *horse crazy— and maybe Trent crazy, too.*

Still, Alexandra drove Trent relentlessly during his lessons. Even if she did like him, she wasn't about to let up on him now.

"How much longer do I have to ride without stirrups?" Trent complained one afternoon when they were working on his posture.

"You want to look good in the horse show, don't you?" Alexandra asked.

Just then Brian rode up on Sinbad. "Aren't you ready to give up on that donkey?" he called to his cousin.

Trent set his jaw and continued posting without his stirrups—once, twice, three more times around the ring. Then he rode out of the ring, his ramrod-straight back showing his resolve.

Good for you, Trent, Alexandra thought, resisting the urge to stick her tongue out at Brian. *Take that, you slimeball!*

After she cooled Pride and rubbed her down, Alexandra bought herself a soda at the vending machine by the barn office. When she saw Trent bring his saddle and bridle into the tack room, she bought another soda for him. "Here," she said, offering him the can. "You deserve it."

"Were you trying to kill me?" Trent asked her as the two of them sat down on a hay bale.

Alexandra watched the blazing sun begin to descend behind the hills. She shook her head. "No, I'm just trying to bring the best out in you."

Trent smiled warmly. "Thanks," he said. Then he was silent for a while. "You know, it's funny," he said finally. "I've spent a lot of time trying to cover up that I cared about doing well at anything. But you and Midnight reminded me that it's okay to let your feelings show once in a while."

He touched Alexandra softly on the sleeve of her denim jacket. Alexandra shivered.

"You know, I'm going to hate going back," he said softly.

"You'll miss Midnight, won't you?" Alexandra's eyes searched his.

"Yeah. A lot," he said. "But I might miss you more."

Alexandra blinked hard. She wouldn't cry. She *wouldn't*. "You scared about the horse show?" she managed to choke out.

Trent shrugged, his face settling into its tough lines once again. But then he softened. "A little. But win or lose, I know I'll come away with something more important. I know that being tough doesn't count with horses . . . or people worth knowing." He reached into his pocket and pulled out a tiny, dark green box. "Go ahead," he said. "Open it. It's for you."

Alexandra looked at Trent, then took the box. She lifted the lid and stared at the tiny gold horseshoe necklace nestled in the cotton.

"Don't ever forget me," he said softly.

How could I? Alexandra wondered silently as she shook her head.

♡ ♡ ♡

The morning of the horse show, Alexandra watched as Trent settled gently into Midnight's saddle. He looked nothing like the tough and wary boy she met only a few weeks ago. Instead, he looked relaxed and confident.

Janine walked up to Alexandra. "Your pupil awaits you," she said. "Wow, he looks like a rider! You've really made a difference with him."

Alexandra nodded. "He *is* a rider. And *he's* the one who made a difference."

"He asked me if I would save Midnight for him when he comes back next summer," Janine added, glancing meaningfully over at Alexandra.

Alexandra smiled. "Well, I'd better go watch him earn that blue ribbon of his," she said.

As she walked toward the ring gate where Trent waited, she touched the lucky horseshoe. She remembered how her body went all tingly when she had let Trent put the necklace around her neck. And now, as she saw the big smile Trent was flashing her, she felt herself going all tingly again. Next summer couldn't possibly come soon enough!

The Love That Almost Wasn't

"I feel rotten," Merilee complained to her friend Annie. They were standing in line with a throng of campers, about to step off a ferry onto Catalina Island.

"I can't believe you got seasick," Annie said. "I love rocky oceans. They're exciting!"

"Well, I could do without that kind of excitement," Merilee said as she hoisted her duffel bag over her shoulder and moved shakily forward. "Look at that poor guy," she whispered, nudging Annie and pointing to a boy leaning unsteadily against the railing. "His face is greener than mine!"

Annie tossed her thick black braid over her shoulder and turned to look. There by the main cabin was a tall, redheaded boy, hanging over the railing. "I'll bet he'll be happy to get off this thing," she said, following his gaze toward the cove where Camp Arroyo was situated.

Taking a deep breath of salty air, Annie was filled with expectation. She'd waited all school year for this week. Camp Arroyo was the first coed camp she'd ever been to, and she was positive it would be a blast. As she stepped onto the wooden dock, her eyes took in the bobbing sailboats, the volleyball court, and the beautiful trees everywhere.

"This way," shouted a couple of tanned, enthusiastic, gorgeous guys with whistles around their necks. They directed Annie and her fellow campers toward the unlit campfire pit.

"Did you see—" Annie started to say to Merilee, but realized her friend had stopped a few feet back and was staring at two guys tossing a Frisbee in a wide grassy area. "Merilee, come on!" she shouted to her friend.

Merilee finally broke her gaze and trotted up to Annie. "Don't you just love going to camp with guys?" she asked breathlessly. "Do you think they're checking us out as much as we're checking them out?"

Annie rolled her eyes. "Probably. But I'm not going to let myself fall for someone I'll never see again."

They dumped their duffel bags in a heap and sat down on the half-log benches surrounding the fire pit.

"Rules and regulations time," groaned a girl behind them. "They go through this every year."

Sure enough, the head counselor started reading off a long list of rules. Annie yawned and stared out at the water lapping gently against the shore. Finally, the counselor moved on to the fun stuff and talked about activities they could sign up for.

"Sailing," Annie whispered to Merilee. "That's what I'm going to do."

"You're on your own, pal." Merilee pretended to gag. "I'm staying on solid ground. Does sunbathing count as an activity?"

"I can't believe you," said Annie, turning her attention back to the counselor. "I want to do so many things I'll never fit them in in just a week."

Next the counselors read the list of cabin assignments. Merilee sighed happily when she heard she and Annie would bunk together. "Cabin 12—I like the sound of that," she said as if tasting the words. "I wonder where it is."

"I hope it's not near any wild boars," said the girl behind Annie.

Annie felt her stomach drop. "Wild boars?" she asked.

Merilee stood up and glared at the girl, then turned back to Annie. "Don't mind her. The campers who've been here before make up stuff to scare new kids like us."

Embarrassed, Annie giggled nervously. "Wild boars," she mumbled.

"All right, everybody," called a counselor. "Take a half hour to store your duffels and get settled. Then report back to the volleyball nets on the beach for a volleyball challenge before dinner."

Somebody let out a whoop of joy and Annie turned to see that it was the redheaded guy she'd seen earlier on the boat. Now he didn't look green at all. He looked tanned—almost golden—and definitely gorgeous.

"Who said we weren't going to get all weird about guys?" Merilee asked, nudging Annie. "Come on. Let's go see our home for the week."

"You go ahead," Annie said. "I want to ask the counselor something." But as soon as Merilee left, Annie stayed where she was and watched a pretty, athletic girl flirting with the guy. Straining, Annie tried to catch their conversation.

"I sure hope we're on the same team, Eric," the girl said.

He grinned at the girl. "It wouldn't be a team without you," he said.

Eric. So that was his name, Annie thought, unconsciously smiling. But in the next instant, she caught herself. He was obviously already taken by that other girl. But it didn't matter. Annie wasn't there to compete for guys, anyway. She walked off toward Cabin 12 and pushed Eric out of her mind.

Half an hour later, she and Merilee were at the volleyball nets. Nick, the head counselor for the boys, had everyone count off to form eight teams. To her delight, Annie found herself on Eric's team. Unfortunately, the girl he'd been talking to earlier was on it, too. Annie saw him wink at her. Angry at herself for getting upset, Annie was silent as the team debated over a name.

"Let's call ourselves the Seals," suggested one girl.

"Way too cute," someone said, imitating a seal sound.

Eric's pretty friend piped up next. "How about the Kona Kannibals?" she suggested.

Eric beamed a smile at the girl. "Way to go, Regan!" he said.

If she wasn't his girlfriend already, she would be soon, Annie thought.

The Kona Kannibals were sent to play the Stingrays. Reluctantly, Annie took her place next to Regan by the net.

The game started slowly, and although the first serve came to Annie, Regan stepped in effortlessly and sent it sailing over the net. Annie bit her lip and tried to concentrate on not wanting to kill her. Regan had it all. She was pretty and athletic, and she had even come up with a great name for the team. But what really bothered Annie was that Regan seemed to have Eric as well. She tried to focus on the game, which was now tied 10–10.

"Great dig!" Eric called as Annie barely got the ball back over the net.

Annie flushed, but quickly told herself that Eric complimented everyone when they made a good hit. He was just friendly, that was all.

Finally, the Kona Kannibals won and the Stingrays walked off defeated.

"Great game," Eric said, falling in stride with Annie as she walked up the path toward her cabin to wash up for dinner.

Say something, Annie commanded herself. But being so close to him had turned her tongue into a useless instrument. She stood there trying to talk, but nothing came out.

For a moment, Eric looked at her strangely, then he flashed a grin. "Well, see you at dinner," he said, and turned toward the boys' cabins.

Annie regained use of her tongue the minute he was gone. "Yes, I'm a geek," she mumbled as she walked into her cabin and plopped on her bunk.

That evening, Annie stole looks at Eric all during dinner. He was at a table with a group of guys and girls that included Regan, and he was making everyone laugh. What a fun guy he was. If only he'd glance her way just once, Annie thought, not knowing what she'd do if he did.

As she sat down on the logs for the evening campfire activities, Annie studied Regan in the firelight and just couldn't stop the flood of jealousy she felt. Why did she have to fall for a guy who obviously liked somebody else? She looked up at the starry sky and began to wish she were home, far away from Eric and Regan and especially from her ridiculous thoughts.

The next morning, everyone signed up for the day's activities. Annie saw Eric in the line for swimming. For a moment she was tempted to join that line, but then she walked determinedly over to the sailing table.

Soon she found herself in a sturdy little boat with a bubbly counselor named Marcia and two campers who looked like twins, named Jane and Jill.

"Ocean's a little restless this morning," Marcia said as they pulled away from the dock. "But we'll have a great time."

Annie lifted her head and let the wind tickle her nose as she listened to Marcia explain how to sail. She had fun learning all the terms and taking her turn at the tiller. Watching the sails billowing in the wind, Annie felt totally relaxed and happy. This was why she'd come to camp, she reminded herself. This was what it was all about.

When they returned to the cove, they saw a big group of people playing on the muddy field just above the beach.

"What's going on?" Jill asked Marcia. "They're all covered with mud!"

"Let's hurry and dock this tub," Marcia said, smiling. "We've got a game of Hold Up the Stage-coach to play!"

After Annie and her fellow sailors had docked and hosed down the little boat, they ran up to the muddy field.

It wasn't long before Annie found herself caught up in the fun, chasing after the player who was carrying the "gold," which was really a bag of mud. Suddenly it was Annie's turn to carry the gold. She cradled the bag close and started to run from a trio of guys, one of whom was Eric. She was just about to tuck and run when Regan ran up beside her.

"Toss it to me," Regan yelled. "I can take it in."

Realizing that Regan was in a better position to score, Annie tossed the muddy sack to her. Regan feinted left, and scored the winning points.

Annie watched miserably as Eric caught Regan up in a muddy hug. "Stupid game," she muttered, going to wash off the mud in the water.

She dunked her head under, and just as she came up, she saw Eric swimming toward her.

"Great handoff," he said, splashing playfully at her.

She gave him a half smile. *He's just being nice,* she thought, as she walked up onto the beach.

"Your name's Annie, isn't it?" he asked, coming up behind her.

Annie nodded. She bent over and flipped her long hair back to help it dry. When she stood up, she found herself staring into Eric's incredible blue eyes. Without thinking, she reached up and wiped a streak of mud off his forehead. He stepped back and looked at her. *Really* looked at her. Horrified that she'd done that, Annie took his look to mean horror, too. Feeling like a complete idiot, she turned and fled toward her cabin. She didn't want to have to hear him say that he already had a girlfriend.

Full of confusion, Annie knew one thing for sure—she couldn't face Eric again. What was he doing talking with her, anyway? He was already going out with another girl. She shot up the path toward her cabin, determined to forget him once and for all.

After dinner that night, Annie and Merilee took their seats around the campfire. It was skit night, and Annie was sure Eric would be right up there, charming everyone, when all she wanted to do was hide. And sure enough, there he was, taking the stage with his buddies. Annie watched as the firelight played on his face, causing shadows to move across his features as he began to do a monologue like a television talk-show host.

"He's so funny," Annie heard Regan say a couple of rows behind her. It was all Annie could do not to turn around and tell her to be quiet.

Once or twice, Annie thought Eric actually glanced her way, but she refused to give him the satisfaction of a smile—especially since he was probably looking past her at Regan.

Merilee nudged her. "What's with you?" she whispered.

Annie shrugged. "Nothing."

But after a while, her resolve started to crack. Eric was clever. Unable to stop herself, Annie began laughing with the rest of the campers.

"That's better," Merilee murmured when Eric left the stage. "I was beginning to think you were in danger of becoming a certified grouch."

♡ ♡ ♡

The week flew by, each day filled with sailing, hiking, swimming, and sing-alongs. Annie kept herself busy, but she still found herself watching Eric from afar. A couple of times he signed up for some of the same activities she did, but Regan was usually not far behind. Once or twice she caught him looking questioningly at her. It was all so puzzling. If he was so tied in with Regan, why was he looking at her? But it didn't really matter anymore. Camp would be over the next day.

"I'm going to miss this place," Merilee said as she sat on her bunk. "Especially all the cute guys."

"Forget the guys," Annie said, a little more strongly than she'd meant to. "It's the sun and the water that *I'm* going to miss." She felt a wave of sadness. She almost wished she had never come here. It was awful to like someone who liked someone else.

The dining hall was actually quiet that night as everyone began to realize they'd be leaving the next morning. Annie stole a look at Eric and felt a lump forming in her throat. Was she going to wonder forever what it would have been like to get to know him?

After dinner, Annie's cabin had cleanup duty. While Merilee scraped plates, Annie took the trash out back.

Dusk was falling as she walked out with two full bags of trash. As she approached the trash cans, she heard a low growl behind her and the hair rose on the back of her neck. When she turned around, she saw a wild boar standing just a few feet away. This boar was no made-up story. It had long yellow tusks and beady eyes that glittered red. Annie's heart was thumping wildly.

"Don't make any sudden moves," said someone behind her. "Set down the bags and back away slowly. He won't hurt you if you don't startle him."

Annie steeled herself not to give way to panic. She turned and saw it was Regan, her eyes riveted on the boar and carrying a thick stick. Doing as she was told, Annie set down the trash and backed toward Regan, half expecting the boar to lunge at them both. Instead, it rummaged around the trash, then lumbered off into the darkness.

The two girls burst into choking sobs that ended up in laughter. Gathering her wits, Annie was finally able to speak. "I'm really glad you showed up," she said. "But why were you here?"

"I was coming to talk to you," Regan said, smiling warmly. "I think you've got the wrong idea about Eric. We're just friends. I wish he liked me, but all he ever talks about is you." She put her arm around Annie's shoulder. "Anyway, I thought you should know that because I think he's too shy to tell you himself."

But just then, Eric walked up. He looked from Annie to Regan, then back to Annie. "I . . . I came to help you with cleanup duty," he said, looking totally embarrassed. Then he turned to Regan. "What are you doing here?"

Regan shrugged and flashed Annie a grin. "Just girl talk," she said. "Anyway, I've got to go pack." As she walked off, she called back, "Hey, Annie, next time you want to go boar hunting, call me!"

Eric looked puzzled. "Boar hunting?"

Annie laughed. "I'll tell you about it sometime."

"Can I tell *you* something right now?" he asked.

Annie nodded. He took her hand and she felt her knees go weak.

Eric shifted from one foot to the other. "You know what I'll miss most about Camp Arroyo?" he asked.

Annie shook her head.

"You," he said.

Annie was thrilled. But then she remembered they'd be leaving in the morning. "I . . . I like you a lot, too," she said, "but I'll never see you again."

Eric broke into a wide grin. "One of my buddies told me that you actually live near me. We're just in different school districts, that's all."

"Really?" said Annie, her thoughts jumping into the future. Now she was sure—her love for Eric was not the love that wasn't, but the love that could be, after all.